I0733481

Plea Of The Damned 4
Forgive Me Kobe

Plea Of The Damned 4
Forgive Me Kobe

Avril Sabine

Cracked Acorn Productions
Australia

Plea Of The Damned 4: Forgive Me Kobe

Published by

Cracked Acorn Productions

PO Box 1365

Gympie, Queensland 4570

Australia

978-1-925617-22-1 (Kindle)

978-1-925617-23-8 (EPUB)

978-1-925617-24-5 (Print)

Genre: Young Adult Urban Fantasy/Paranormal

Copyright 2017 © Avril Sabine

Cover design by Caitlyn Petersen

All rights reserved

*For those who stand by their friends, no
matter what they must face.*

Plea Of The Damned

Have you ever done something and immediately wished you could undo it? Jack knows that feeling very well. He's damned, bound to haunt his old school and help students until he atones for his sins. It's the last thing he wants to do. But since the alternative is an eternity in hell, he's not about to say no.

Book 4: Forgive Me Kobe

In an effort to salvage a friendship, Kobe turns up at school after dark. Things rapidly go wrong and he's held at gunpoint, along with his friend Xavier, fearing he'll lose more than a friendship. When a ghost offers to help, Kobe doesn't know if he's lost his mind, has already died or if ghosts might actually be real. And if ghosts are real, how can one help him and Xavier escape from the gunmen?

*

This story was written by an Australian author using Australian spelling.

Chapter One

Jack

Jack Richards walked past a classroom, glancing inside. It was Friday afternoon, about twenty-five minutes until the bell rang and the students were restless. They checked the time, glanced at friends and whispered to those seated beside them when the teacher wasn't looking. He didn't blame them for wanting to get out of this place. He'd wanted to leave decades ago. It probably didn't help that the September holidays weren't that far away.

Passing another classroom, he looked inside, his gaze drawn to Lucy, the first student he'd helped. He couldn't believe he'd been able to help any of the kids. Each time he'd been asked to help a kid, he'd been sure he'd fail. Believing the angel had deliberately set him up to fail so he couldn't atone for his sins. Every single sin. The major and the minor ones. Not that he'd been asked to help often. At this rate, he'd be stuck as a ghost for centuries.

He wore his leather jacket over his white t-shirt, even though he couldn't feel the chill of the early spring afternoon. It wasn't like he had anything else to wear. This was it. The clothes he'd died in. Walking past another classroom, he looked in at the students, half of them peering out the far windows where they would be able to see the cricket field that also doubled as an athletics track. At this time of year the athletics team had it to themselves since cricket season didn't start until next month. Neither sport had ever interested him, much to his father's disappointment. He'd played a bit of cricket, before everything went wrong, a casual game with friends rather than caring either way about winning or losing.

Jack turned his back on the classroom, seeing more classrooms across a grassed area, sighing heavily. It had been months since he'd helped Aiden. It'd take him decades to atone for his major sins, let alone his minor ones. About to stride through the school grounds to the groundsman's shed before the bell rang, movement caught his attention. He spun to see the angel. He bit back the first comment that came to mind, determined not to antagonise him. Maybe then the angel would actually be helpful.

"No sarcastic greeting?" the angel asked.

Jack pressed his lips together, barely keeping yet another sarcastic comment to himself. When he thought he might be over the urge to blurt it out, he spoke. "Who do you want me to help this time?"

The angel looked past Jack to the classroom and waited for Jack to face the window before he pointed to first one student and then another. "Kobe and Xavier."

Jack stared at the boys for a moment, an entire classroom separating them. "Two? I'm meant to help two?"

"Are you saying you refuse?"

He opened his mouth to protest the unfairness of it. Something in the angel's tone and expression kept him quiet. He had a feeling refusing wasn't an option. That he wouldn't like the consequences. "Are you going to give me more than names this time?"

The angel's lips curved into his usual angelic smile. "Haven't we been over this before?"

Jack's hands tightened into fists as he held back an angry retort. "You think that's fair? Giving me two at once with no extra help. I should get twice the amount of information I normally get." Not that a single name was much information.

"You could say that you have gained twice the usual information. Did I not give you two names?"

Jack pressed his lips together again, desperately trying not to say the angry words that wanted to escape. When he finally spoke, the word was abrupt. "Yes."

"You have gained the chance to atone for your sins, that's more than many are given. What about the ones who believe it unfair you've been given this chance? Should we have listened to them?"

He shook his head, not knowing what to say. All he wanted to do was beg for the names of the ones who didn't want him to have a chance. He had a bad feeling one of them was Rose. Not that he blamed her since he'd been the one responsible for her death. He gestured towards the classroom. "I want them to have a chance." More of a chance than he'd had.

"Do you want them to have a chance or is it that you want to atone for your sins so you can finally leave here."

It surprised him that he actually did want them to have a chance. After the ones he'd helped, he'd started paying attention to what was going on around the school. At times wishing he could warn Lucy and

Jena against false friends and wanting Aiden to attend the school so he could see how he was going. "I care."

The angel stared at him for a moment. "I believe you might actually care. That is a surprise."

Before he could protest the angel's words, and the tone he'd used, the angel vanished. "Blasted bird." He should have known nothing he did would impress the angel. How was he meant to help two kids? It looked like the angel was determined to see him fail. It wasn't like he could be in two places at once.

He stared at the boys. The one sitting closest to him, Xavier, was dark haired with brown eyes, olive skin and a square jaw. He'd seen him playing footy and he certainly had the build for it. Kobe had sandy brown hair, hazel eyes and a narrower jaw, anger in his gaze whenever it was drawn to Xavier.

As if feeling Kobe's gaze on him, Xavier looked over. Seeing the anger in Xavier's eyes, a far greater one than that of Kobe's, Jack had a feeling this assignment wasn't going to be simple. Xavier had looked murderous. That was all he needed.

Sighing heavily Jack turned to lean against the wall, even though he couldn't feel it. Habits were hard to break, even after decades. What did the angel expect him to do? Prevent them from killing each other? He heard again the echoing memory of the gunshot that had ended Rose's life. He wasn't about to let that happen again. Not at his school.

Chapter Two

Kobe

Kobe looked away from Xavier. It had been weeks and still his supposed best friend looked like he hated him. How many times did he have to tell him it hadn't been his fault? It wasn't like he'd gone after Clara. He checked the time. Only minutes until school was done for the week. He couldn't wait. School had become unbearable since Clara had ruined things between them.

Once more he glanced at Xavier, who was staring out the window. They'd been best friends since grade four when they'd both started school on the same day, halfway through the year. Nothing had come between them for more than a day or two. Until Clara.

The bell ringing had Kobe gathering his books and

rushing towards the door. He was held up by a group of girls pushing past him. About to step through the door, Xavier shouldered into him, not glancing in his direction or apologising.

Kobe rubbed his shoulder, stepping through the doorway to glare after Xavier. For a moment he nearly walked away. But he couldn't bring himself to throw away years of friendship over a single incident. They'd been nine-years-old when they'd met and had been best friends for the past seven years. It was his longest ever friendship. Taking a deep breath, he strode after Xavier. He caught up with him at his locker.

Xavier opened the locker, barely glancing at Kobe.

"How long are you going to hate me?"

Xavier rummaged in his locker.

"I didn't kiss her. She was the one who kissed me. I didn't know she was interested." Why couldn't Xavier believe him?

Xavier slammed the locker door shut, shoving books into his backpack.

"Come on, Xavier. How could I have expected her to kiss me? It's not something that happens all the time." He followed Xavier as he strode towards the front gate, along with the students heading in that direction. "Xavier." He rested a hand on his friend's shoulder.

Xavier shrugged him off, glaring at him. "Doesn't happen all the time?"

Kobe tried not to smile as he remembered the two girls who'd kissed him. One had been last year, one earlier this year. "Those ones weren't exactly unexpected. But Clara's kiss was. I barely talked to her. You were the one who did most of the talking."

"Yeah, right. She wouldn't have kissed you without encouragement."

Kobe tried not to sigh. They were back to the same accusations that led nowhere. It was time to try something different. "How can I make it up to you?"

"You can't." Xavier didn't slow his stride.

"There must be something I can do. What if I talk her into going on a date with you?"

"You think I want her after she's kissed you?"

Once again he almost gave up, wanting to throw his hands in the air and tell Xavier that he was meant to trust him. Meant to believe what he said. Weren't they supposed to be friends? "Fine. Forget about Clara. What can I do?"

Xavier stopped abruptly, facing Kobe, the crowd walking around them. "Meet me behind the athletics shed in an hour."

Kobe didn't like the speculative look on Xavier's face. Xavier wanted revenge. He couldn't blame him, except for the fact he was innocent of the accusation. "I can't. I have to babysit my sister."

"Should have known you'd come up with some lame excuse." Xavier continued towards the front gate.

Kobe watched him walk away, sighing heavily he hurried after him. Seven years of friendship had to be worth at least one more attempt at fixing things between them. "Once Mum is home. She'll be home at six-thirty. I can meet you back here about fifteen or twenty minutes after that."

Xavier stopped again. "You'll meet me after dark."

Kobe nodded, wanting to get this over and done with. "Yeah. At a quarter to seven." The speculative look was back on his friend's face. There was sure to be humiliation involved and probably a recording of the moment so everyone would have the chance to see what had happened.

Xavier smiled. "I'll see you then."

Kobe stared after Xavier, wondering if they'd ever be friends again. Especially after whatever Xavier had planned for him. There was a good chance he might be the one glaring at Xavier with the murderous look his friend kept solely for him. He had to be crazy. Or a glutton for punishment. He wanted things back the way they'd been before Clara had ruined them.

Spotting Clara several metres away, he hurried through the school gates and headed in the direction of his sister's primary school. One person angry with him was bad enough. He didn't need Imogen annoyed with him too. She was sure to retaliate and for a ten-year-old she could be pretty inventive when it came to revenge. It was a good thing she wasn't helping Xavier with whatever he was planning.

Imogen was impatiently waiting for him at the front of her school, standing with a cluster of her friends who also waited to be collected. She had the same hazel coloured eyes that he did, her hair a lighter brown, plaited back from her face, wisps escaping. There was a scattering of freckles across her nose and cheeks and she talked non-stop about her day. Luckily she didn't need more than the occasional indistinct murmur or nod. He was too busy trying to figure out what Xavier might have planned for him.

He frowned as he pictured the area. Trees lined the fence near the athletics shed, reducing visibility from the road. There weren't as many trees as there were in some of the areas of the school, such as near the groundsman's shed, so they'd be less hidden from the road. Maybe that was part of the plan. Xavier might have someone across the road waiting to record whatever he was planning. There was always plenty of light on the cricket field, some of the spotlights remaining on all night, every night.

During the walk home, Kobe changed his mind several times, alternating between meeting Xavier and not turning up. Reaching home he opened the door and reminded his sister to start her homework, before heading to his bedroom. He closed the door, dropping his backpack onto the floor. If he wanted to salvage their friendship he had to meet Xavier. There was no choice in the matter.

Images rushed through his mind. Ones from the past seven years. For a moment, anger raced through him and his hands tightened into fists. Xavier should have known he never would have gone after Clara. He should have trusted him. Breathing out slowly, he focused on letting the anger go. It took several minutes before he could move away from the door, the urge to hit something fading. He'd meet with Xavier. Give their friendship one last chance. It was up to Xavier after that. If he really valued their friendship then he wouldn't do something to make it impossible for them to remain friends.

He rummaged in his backpack. First he needed to get homework done or his mum wouldn't let him go anywhere. He left his books on his desk and grabbed a snack before returning to the desk to start his homework.

When Kobe eventually heard his mum's car pull up out the front, he leaned back from his desk, stretching. He glanced down. He'd planned to get changed before his mum arrived home. Rising from the desk, he smiled ruefully. He'd also expected to have his homework finished. It was close to done. Hopefully close enough his mum wouldn't send him back to finish it off.

After changing into jeans and a t-shirt, grabbing a hoodie since it was likely to be cool outside, he slipped his phone into a pocket of his jeans and went to look for his mum. He found her cornered in the hallway, Imogen trying to show her an assignment she received an 'A' for, looking tired.

Maria looked towards him. She had the same hazel coloured eyes as both of her children and hair similar in colour to her daughter's, cut short rather than falling past her shoulders. Her gaze was drawn back to Imogen. "Do you think you can tell me about it after dinner?"

Kobe tugged his sister out of the way. "Let Mum in the house, why don't you?"

Maria's gaze was drawn back to Kobe. "Why are

you dressed to go out?" She nodded towards the hoodie he'd put on, leaving it unzipped.

"I'm going to catch up with Xavier." He ushered Imogen ahead of him as he walked towards the kitchen.

"Your fight is over?" Maria asked.

Kobe shrugged. "I guess we'll soon see."

Maria stared at Kobe for a moment, stopping in the doorway of the kitchen. "What is going on?"

He shrugged again. "We're going to talk."

Maria smiled. "I'm glad. I know how much it's bothered you."

"Yeah, well." He shrugged again.

"Can I go too?" Imogen demanded.

"What about dinner?" Maria asked Kobe.

"I'll have something later." He crossed the kitchen and grabbed a green apple from the fruit basket sitting on the kitchen bench. "Xavier wanted to meet earlier."

"Have you done your homework?"

"Did you hear me?" Imogen stepped in front of Kobe. "I want to go too."

Kobe messed her hair. "As if we'd get any talking done. You never shut up."

"I do." Imogen glared at him.

"Don't tease your sister." Maria opened the fridge,

glancing over her shoulder. "Homework?" She took out some vegetables, placing them at the side of the sink.

"Pretty much. About half an hour should have it finished." He took a bite of the apple.

"Not too late." Maria pointed a warning finger at him. "And no wandering the streets. Straight to Xavier's and straight back afterwards."

Swallowing his mouthful, he scowled at her. "I'm not a little kid, Mum." He slowly shook his head. "Not like Imogen." He turned to leave the room, about to take another bite of his apple.

"Oh no you don't," Maria called out at the same time as Imogen complained that she wasn't a little kid.

He turned with a grin, seeing her tap her cheek with a forefinger. "It's not like I'm going away for a week or anything," he muttered. Reaching his mum's side, he kissed the spot she'd indicated before striding towards the doorway.

"And stop hassling your sister."

Stepping through the doorway, he raised a hand, not bothering to look over his shoulder. "See you later." Taking another bite of the apple he strode for the front door, slipping his feet into his sneakers before stepping outside. The breeze was cool and he was glad he'd grabbed a hoodie.

Chapter Three

Kobe

Kobe couldn't stop wondering what Xavier had planned. Surely he wouldn't go too far. Images again raced through his mind. They'd always been there for each other. Finishing the apple, he tossed it under a shrub, crossing the street after waiting for a car to drive past.

It didn't take long to reach the school and walk around the outskirts, jumping the fence when he neared the athletics shed. The trees created lengthy shadows, preventing the streetlights from casting light on the school grounds. There were lights further away on the cricket field, but between him and the shed was only darkness. Anything could be there.

Again he hesitated. What did Xavier have planned? Taking a deep breath, he forced himself to walk towards the shed, reaching for his phone as he did so. He didn't get the chance to take it out of his pocket before Xavier spoke. He left his phone where it was, his empty hand curling into a fist at the tone Xavier used.

"I didn't think you'd come."

Kobe spun to face the trees along the fence line, Xavier little more than an indistinct shadow. "Why wouldn't I? We're friends, aren't we?" He forced himself to relax, uncurling his hand.

"Supposed to be."

Kobe bit back the words he wanted to speak. Arguing it hadn't been his fault hadn't made any difference. "Why did you want to meet here?" He was tempted to take out his phone to use the flashlight app to check Xavier's expression. More than likely it matched his own.

"You're going to run around the track naked."

Kobe watched the indistinct figure of Xavier stride towards the athletics shed. Had he heard right? Surely Xavier didn't expect that of him. That was cruel. He thought back to earlier in the year when he'd told Xavier about the nightmare he'd had of running around the track and realising he wore no clothes, everyone laughing at him as he continued to run. There was no way he was going to do that. Hurrying after Xavier, he placed a hand on his supposed friend's shoulder. "No."

Xavier shrugged his hand off. "You want to make it up to me, that's what you've got to do." Xavier continued towards the shed.

Kobe looked between Xavier and the fence he'd jumped over, his hands curling into fists. Maybe seven years of friendship weren't worth fighting for. Forcing his hands to relax again, and letting his breath out slowly, he strode after Xavier. "It goes both ways."

Xavier stopped at the side of the athletics shed. "What does?"

"Friendship. You should have believed me. Running naked around the track has nothing to do with proving anything. It's only about humiliating me."

"And you didn't humiliate me?" Xavier demanded.

"I–" Kobe broke off when a shout came from the cricket field. He looked in the direction of the shout. Three men ran towards them, the lights at the far side of the field highlighting them. One was in the lead, two following him.

"What is going–"

Catching a glimpse of a knife held by one of the men giving chase, Kobe tried to cover Xavier's mouth. He half managed, his hand angling across his friend's face. "Quiet."

Xavier pushed him away. "What is-"

"He has a knife." Kobe kept his voice low, turning to face the men who ran towards them. "We need to-" He broke off when the two men tackled the third to the ground.

"I warned you," the man with the knife said.

Kobe took a step backwards. If it had been daylight, the men were close enough they would have seen them. It was only the shadows keeping them safe. He took another step, noticing the shadowy figure of Xavier did the same.

"It wasn't me, Alvin. I didn't tell anyone." The man struggled to escape. His fist connected with a jaw.

Alvin retaliated, using the hand that held the knife.

The third man stumbled back. "You killed Walter."

Kobe froze. Blood spread across the t-shirt, the colour stark against the light colour of the fabric. Beside him he heard Xavier's indrawn breath.

"Shut up, Declan." Alvin pointed at the man as he continued to back away, using the hand that held the blood stained knife.

Declan glanced around the area. "We have to get out of here."

"You will not move." Alvin again used the knife to point at Declan, who froze.

"We have to get out of here." Kobe echoed Declan's words, backing away.

"I… he…" Xavier's voice trailed off.

Kobe knew exactly how his friend felt. The moment didn't feel real. A crack sounded from beside him and he froze, holding his breath.

"Sorry." Xavier eased off the stick he'd stood on, the cracking sound coming softer.

"Someone's over there." Alvin spun to face their direction.

Kobe grabbed Xavier's arm. "Run." He dragged his friend with him. Something flew past, hitting a tree ahead of them.

"Stop or I'll shoot you," Alvin called out.

Had that been a bullet? Kobe came to a stumbling stop, continuing to hold Xavier's arm.

"Don't move," Alvin ordered.

Kobe didn't know if he could have moved even if he'd been ordered to. What did it feel like to be shot? He hadn't heard the sound of a gun being fired. Did that mean it had a silencer? Not that he knew anything about guns and silencers other than what he'd seen on television.

"Tie their hands," Alvin said.

"What with?" Declan demanded.

"I don't know. Find something." Alvin barely paused before speaking again. "I'm warning you. Don't move."

Kobe had remained perfectly still so could only assume the order had been directed at Xavier. He tightened his grip on his friend's arm, wanting to tell him not to do anything stupid.

"It's dark."

There was a whiny quality to Declan's voice that reminded Kobe of his sister when she didn't want to do something. His chest tightened at the thought of Imogen wanting to come with him. There'd been a few times he'd taken his sister along when he and Xavier had gone somewhere she liked to go.

"Do I have to do everything?" Alvin demanded. "Use their shoelaces. Show some initiative. And put that torch away. There's more than enough light around here."

Declan stopped in front of Kobe, tugging on his laces, muttering under his breath about the knots. Kobe fought the urge to kick Declan in the face. He couldn't outrun a bullet. Nor did he know how many bullets were in a gun. He doubted Alvin had a simple six shooter that would need to be reloaded after being fired half a dozen times.

"Put your hands out." Declan rose to his feet, remaining in front of Kobe. He tied the laces tightly around Kobe's wrists as soon as he held out his hands. "I don't know how long the laces will hold."

"They'll hold long enough for us to figure out something better to keep them from running to the cops," Alvin said.

Once he'd tied Kobe's hands together, Declan turned towards Xavier and removed his shoelaces, tying them around Xavier's wrists. "They'll have phones."

"Then take them." Alvin's tone was filled with exaggerated patience. "What's wrong with kids these days? Who wants to hang out at school once you're done with it for the day?"

"I used to-"

Alvin interrupted Declan. "Quit talking and get their phones."

Worried about Alvin's short temper, Kobe spoke. "In the back pocket of my jeans."

Declan took the phone, turning it off and tossing it towards the athletics shed before facing Xavier. "And yours?"

"I... It was confiscated. In last class today."

Kobe knew for a fact that was a lie. "He was caught

sending a text to his girlfriend. The teacher read it out to the entire class."

"Teachers." Declan said the word like it was a curse. "Always on a power trip."

"Check him," Alvin ordered. "Make sure he isn't lying."

Kobe wanted to point out that if anyone was on a power trip, it was Alvin. He pressed his lips together so the words didn't escape, reminding himself he couldn't outrun a bullet.

"What are we going to do with them?"

"Find a building to shut them in. Or maybe a cupboard they can be locked in," Alvin said. "Give us time to wait for our contact to arrive so we can get out of town. This place has been quiet for the past two weeks. Should have known something'd go wrong tonight."

"Everything will be locked," Declan said.

No one would find them until Monday. Or longer if they were locked up somewhere that wasn't used every day. And he hadn't told anyone where he was going. Kobe didn't want to risk being locked up that long. "There's a security system. If you break into the buildings a silent alarm will go off." Although there'd been problems with the system and it didn't always work reliably. Some mornings classroom doors were found unlocked and no alarms had been set off.

Alvin stepped in front of them. "Why would you help us?"

"I don't want to get shot. Or caught in a shootout between you and the police." Kobe tried to see Alvin's gun. It was impossible to see it in the shadows.

"Right." Alvin paused a moment. "You find some rope, drag Walter into the shadows and meet me near that little shed in the north east corner. We'll tie them to one of the trees over there. Plenty of trees to hide them from the road."

"Where will I find rope?" Declan asked.

Alvin gave him a slap across the ear. "Use your brain. Now get moving. We have things to sort out."

"I think there's a couple of pieces in the car. I'll see if they're long enough." Declan hurried away.

Alvin sighed heavily. "Don't know why I bother with him. More trouble than he's worth." He paused a moment. "Right." There was another pause. "You two start moving. I'm sure you know the building I'm talking about."

"The groundsman's shed?" Xavier asked.

"How would I know?" Alvin gestured in the direction, his knife catching the limited light.

Chapter Four

Kobe

Kobe stared at the knife. Alvin's other hand was empty. Where was the gun? Not knowing for certain if Alvin had a gun, he walked in the direction Alvin had indicated. "What are you planning to do to us?"

"If you behave, nothing. We'll be out of here not long after midnight." Alvin walked behind them.

"Why not leave now?" Kobe found it odd to walk in his sneakers without the laces keeping the top from gaping, but it wasn't as bad as he'd feared.

"Stop talking," Alvin ordered.

They remained silent, only the sound of their footsteps and the occasional stick breaking when one of them stepped on it. For a moment Kobe wished he attended a tree free school. One filled with concrete or pavers. Although summer would be a killer with the amount of heat that reflected off concrete. He glanced towards Xavier, noticing his friend do the same.

"No talking," Alvin warned.

"I wasn't planning to," Kobe said.

"You better not have."

"I was thinking how this served Xavier right for making me meet him here."

"This is your fault," Xavier muttered. "You were the one who kissed Clara."

"You were the one who wanted me to run naked around the cricket field while you recorded it," Kobe said.

"Recorded it with what?" Alvin demanded.

Kobe instantly regretted his words. Xavier wasn't meant to have a phone. He had no idea what he'd done with it, but it hadn't been confiscated. "That's the worst part. He was expecting to use my phone. So much for being my friend."

"You stole his girlfriend?" Alvin asked.

"As if. He only wished she was his girlfriend." Kobe hoped that if Alvin got to know them he'd be less likely to want to kill them. Although that hadn't really helped Walter. Then he remembered Xavier was meant to already have a girlfriend. "Not that it matters. He ended up with another girl a couple of weeks later."

Alvin laughed. "What's your name, girlfriend stealer?"

"Kobe."

"Bit of a lady's man, are you?"

"Nah. If I was, I'd be able to figure out how to keep a girlfriend for longer than a month."

Alvin chuckled again. "And you? Xavier was it?"

Xavier mumbled something that could have been an agreement.

"Why didn't you go after your girl before she became interested in someone else?"

"Because he stuttered every time he tried to talk to her." Kobe grinned, feeling like Xavier deserved the comment after what he'd tried to do.

"I did not," Xavier protested, repeating the words when Alvin laughed at him.

"This one probably won't last long. She complains you never talk to her," Kobe said.

"You're as bad as Declan. Although he's never had a girlfriend. Completely freezes whenever a woman looks at him."

"I can talk to girls," Xavier muttered.

"Just not the ones you're interested in." Kobe felt a perverse kind of satisfaction at that comment. How could Xavier have expected him to live out his worst nightmare?

When the area grew too dark to see anything Alvin turned on a torch, pointing it ahead of them, his fingers covering most of the light so only a little escaped. "Stand against that tree there." He used the light to show a tree near the groundsman's shed. "And don't try anything."

Kobe leaned against the tree, wishing he could break the shoelaces wrapped several times around his wrists. Declan had tied them too tight. He kept his gaze on Alvin when Xavier stood beside him, shoulder to shoulder. He almost glanced at his friend. Did he have a plan? Were they still friends? But Alvin continued to watch them. He didn't dare look at Xavier or talk to him.

Time stretched out and Kobe tried to speak, Alvin telling him to be quiet before he'd barely said a word. He had no idea if his earlier words had helped. Nor did he know if Alvin had a gun. He hadn't seen one. So what had flown past them? Had it been a bullet?

Declan came out of the shadows, stumbling over sticks and swearing when he ran into a tree, Alvin shining the torch on him. Declan shaded his eyes, several lengths of rope in his other hand. "I thought we couldn't use a torch."

"Tie them to that tree. No one will notice us in here. Not with all these trees. What did you do with Walter?"

Declan wrapped the rope around their waists and the tree, tying a knot and letting the other pieces of rope fall to the ground before he faced Alvin. "What do you mean?"

"I told you to drag Walter into the shadows." Alvin said the words slowly and with exaggerated patience.

"Didn't you do that?"

Alvin took a deep breath, slowly letting it out, exaggerating the action. "I asked you to drag Walter into the shadows. Why would I ask you to do something and then do it myself? Now go and do it."

"He wasn't there. Thought that meant you'd done it."

"What do you mean he wasn't there?" Alvin pointed the torch at Declan's face, sliding his fingers back to allow a full beam of light to escape.

Declan blinked rapidly, shielding his eyes. "Only the blood. He was missing. I thought you'd dragged him away."

Kobe strained at the ropes, wanting to escape while Alvin and Declan were distracted. They were too tight.

Alvin lowered the torch, his fingers covering most of the light again. "He's alive?"

Declan shrugged.

"We have to find him. Before he escapes or tries to come after us," Alvin said.

"What if he rings the police?" Declan asked.

"He's not likely to do that. He's as caught up in this as we are." Alvin pointed the knife at Declan. "Stay here. Watch the kids. They would call the police." He shined the torch at a watch on his wrist. "Less than four hours until midnight. Then we can get out of here." Alvin strode through the trees, heading back the way they'd come.

Declan took out a torch, turning it on before the light from Alvin's torch was out of view.

Kobe stared after Alvin. "What is Walter likely to do?"

"Don't talk." Declan glanced around the area, his torch travelling the same path as his gaze. "Alvin wouldn't want you to talk."

Kobe caught sight of something, or someone, standing beside the groundsman's shed. "Wait. What was that?"

"Where?" Declan shined the torch back across the same path.

"There. Beside the shed," Xavier said.

Declan shined the light of his torch on a young man standing beside the shed, his arms crossed. "What am I meant to be looking at?"

The young man had black hair, wore a white t-shirt with a black leather jacket and blue denim jeans, looking like he'd stepped out of an old movie. He grinned, dark eyes staring at Declan. "He can't see me." He stepped away from the shed, uncrossing his arms. "I'm Jack." The young man walked forward and straight through Declan, who was trying to figure out what they were looking at.

Chapter Five

Kobe stared at Jack, mouth open. "Did you see that?" His voice was little more than a whisper.

"He walked through Declan. Do you think we're dead?" Xavier asked.

Declan spun to face them. "Are you playing a joke on me? I can't see anyone."

"I'd tell him it was an owl and it flew away. You don't want to go upsetting him," Jack said.

"An owl." Kobe barely managed to speak the words.

"Flew away," Xavier added.

None of this could be possible. Kobe stared at Jack, wanting to ask him what was going on. But Declan eyed them suspiciously. He needed to get Declan to move further away so he wouldn't hear them whispering. "Can you untie us? We won't run off. Let us stay near the shed over there. We're out in the open here. Does Walter have a gun?"

Declan took a step backwards. "No." He took another step. "I don't think so."

"Good plan," Jack said. "Find out what he knows about Walter."

"Are you sure?" Xavier asked.

"How well do you know him?" Kobe glanced at Jack, who nodded encouragingly. "Are you friends?"

"Not that being friends means anything." Xavier sent a daggered look towards Kobe. "They're just as likely to stab you in the back. Or kiss the girl you like."

Declan now stood with his back against the wall of the shed, the light of the torch directed towards Kobe. "That's wrong. Friends don't do that to each other."

Kobe breathed out heavily. "I didn't kiss her. She kissed me."

"She did?" Declan asked.

"Keep him talking," Jack said. "He might let something slip."

Kobe had no idea why he obeyed a group hallucination, but he did. "I don't even like her. The girl I liked dumped me. Said I had no idea how to be a good boyfriend."

Declan slowly lowered the torch. "I have no idea either."

"Said I should be dating Xavier since I always put him first. But we've been mates since we were nine."

"She said that?" Xavier sounded surprised.

Kobe shrugged. He hadn't wanted to tell him at the time. Didn't want him to feel guilty. "It wasn't like it was your fault. I could have said no each time you wanted to go somewhere."

"Keep him talking. I'll see what Alvin is up to and try to find Walter." Jack strode away.

Kobe wanted to call him back. He shrugged again. "It didn't seem right to ditch you because I had someone else in my life and she didn't want to go to any of the places you invited me."

"I'm sorry," Xavier said. "You really didn't kiss Clara, did you?"

"That's what I've been trying to tell you for weeks." He didn't bother keeping the exasperation from his voice.

A sound had Declan shining his torch in that direction.

"Lower the torch," Alvin demanded. "Are you trying to blind me?"

Declan lowered the torch. "Did you find Walter?"

"Does it look like I found him?" Alvin demanded.

"I don't know."

"Use your brain. I don't know why I bother." Alvin turned to Kobe and Xavier. "If either of you try and escape, I will come after you." He pointed the knife at them in warning.

Kobe noticed that most of the blood was cleaned off the blade. He didn't know if that made it better or worse. "We're tied up. How are we meant to escape?"

"Good." Alvin turned back to Declan. "Right." He paused a moment. "You check the area around the cricket field, I'll check the buildings past it. We need to find Walter before he does something stupid." Alvin started to walk away, turning back before he'd got far. "Hurry up."

Declan gestured towards Kobe and Xavier. "Is it okay to leave-"

"Now, Declan." Alvin's words were sharp. He strode away, obviously expecting Declan to follow.

With one more glance towards the boys, Declan hurried after Alvin, the light going with them.

Kobe wished one of them could have left a torch behind. "Did you see Jack?"

"How can he be real? He walked right through Declan."

"That'd be because I'm a ghost." Jack's voice came from in front of them.

Kobe's heart leapt. "Couldn't you have given us some kind of warning that you were back? Like make a sound or something."

"Did you miss the part where I said I'm a ghost?" Jack asked dryly.

"We're dead, aren't we," Xavier said.

"I have no idea what's going on." And he really wished he did. "But I do know we need to find a way to get out of here. Before Alvin or Declan come back or Walter finds us." He'd worry about being able to see Jack once they were safe.

"The one you really have to worry about is Walter. He has a gun, is injured and is looking for Alvin," Jack said. "It's not a bad wound, but it will need dealing with before he loses too much blood. I caught him examining it and muttering that he must have passed out from shock, not pain. Sounded like he was trying to convince himself."

"Doesn't Alvin have a gun too?" Xavier asked.

"Slingshot," Jack said. "Can you sit down? There's a piece of broken glass you could use to cut the rope."

"How are we meant to find it in the dark?" Xavier demanded.

"I can guide you," Jack said. "I can move your hand to the glass."

Kobe tried to sit down, using his bound hands to

push at the rope around their waists. "I saw you walk straight through Declan. How can you guide us?" The rope tightened. "Xavier, help me push the rope down so we can sit."

Xavier helped. "I don't know why you're bothering. It's pointless. We can't see, Jack is either a ghost or we're both hallucinating and there's an angry man with a gun wandering around the school grounds. An injured, angry man."

Kobe tried to see his friend. Xavier was right. It was dark enough that all the shadows blended into each other and although there was some light that could be seen through the trees, it didn't penetrate to where they were. "What do you want to do? Sit here and hope no one shoots us?"

"No."

"Then what?" Anger rushed through Kobe. If it hadn't been for Xavier they wouldn't be in this situation. A few seconds later his anger faded. He'd chosen to meet Xavier. He was equally at fault.

"I don't know. But there has to be something more logical than listening to a ghost."

"Until you figure it out, I'll go with Jack's plan." He paused a moment. "Where's the glass?" He sat on the ground, the rope tighter than it had been before.

"Here."

He felt Jack's hand on his, guiding it to the cold shard. The hand felt as real as his. How could Jack be a ghost? "You're going to have to help me find the best place to cut the rope. I wouldn't want to cut either of us."

"You better not," Xavier muttered.

Once Jack had positioned his hand, he sawed against the rope. "Where's your phone?"

Xavier didn't answer immediately. "I put it on the roof of the athletics shed and set it to record."

Chapter Six

Kobe

Kobe stopped, once again trying to see his friend in the dark. "You recorded Alvin stabbing Walter?"

"I'd planned to record you and upload it to Youtube."

"But you recorded them." He felt Xavier shrug beside him.

"I guess so. I don't know how good it will be."

Kobe sawed at the rope again. "We have to get your phone."

"Forget the phone," Jack said. "The pair of you need to get out of here the moment you're free."

"We have to at least get my phone." Kobe felt the rope give slightly. "There's enough information on it they could figure out where I live."

"Are you out of your tree?" Jack demanded.

"Walter has a gun, Alvin has a knife that he doesn't mind using and Declan is willing to do anything Alvin asks of him. The moment you're free you need to make tracks."

Kobe couldn't help thinking about Imogen. Her constant chatter, the eyes so much like his and his mum's and the scattering of freckles. There was no way he'd lead three criminals back to his place. Particularly since one of them had a gun. "I need to get my phone first."

"Do you know why I was sent to help you?" Jack demanded.

"Of course we don't," Xavier said.

"Judging by the previous ones I've helped, there's a good chance either of you might die."

Jack's words caused Kobe's chest to tighten and his hand to slow. He drew in an unsteady breath. "Xavier can go home, but I need to get my phone. My sister is ten. Do you think I'd lead someone, with a gun, to her?"

"Blasted angel," Jack muttered.

"Angel?" Xavier asked.

That had been what Kobe had been about to ask. Surely Jack didn't expect them to believe angels were real too. "Why are you a ghost?" He hissed as the glass nicked his finger, a trickle of blood making it difficult to grip the shard.

"What happened?" Xavier asked.

"Nothing." Kobe tried to see Jack. It was still impossible. "Why are you a ghost, Jack? And why are you helping us?"

"I have to atone for my sins. Can you do that any quicker? One of them is likely to be back before you cut through the rope."

Kobe grit his teeth. Jack obviously didn't realise how difficult this was. The rope gave a little more.

"You must have done something pretty major if you've got to atone for it," Xavier said.

"We don't have time to talk. You have to escape," Jack said.

"Like we can go anywhere when we're tied up," Kobe said dryly. "Why do you keep avoiding the question?"

"I shot someone."

Kobe's fingers slipped and he nearly cut himself. "You expect us to trust you when you killed someone?"

"That is why I try and avoid this. If you don't trust me, then you're likely to be killed," Jack said.

"Who did you kill?" Xavier asked.

There was a lengthy silence before Jack replied. "Rose. My girlfriend."

"It gets even better," Kobe muttered.

"You have to be kidding," Xavier exclaimed. "How are you any better than Alvin?"

Once again Jack didn't answer immediately. "I like to think there are a lot of differences. I didn't set out to deliberately hurt anyone, least of all the one I love."

The rope gave and Kobe leapt to his feet, looking towards where Xavier should be. "We need light so I can see to cut through the shoelaces."

"Forget about the laces. Run," Jack said. "Walter isn't that far from here."

Kobe shook his head at Jack's words. "Then we go towards the cricket field and get our phones." He took a step in the direction he thought was the right one, continuing to hold the glass shard.

"Did you listen to anything I said?" Jack demanded.

"It doesn't change anything." Kobe took an unsteady step forward, the darkness disorientating.

"You're not making it easy for me to help you," Jack said.

"You could scout ahead for us." Kobe stumbled on a stick, his grip on the shard momentarily tightening. He relaxed his grip. A serious cut was the last thing he needed.

"We should call the cops," Xavier said.

"How?" Both their phones were on the other side of the school and getting over the fence with their hands tied together would be impossible.

"I don't know," Xavier said. "We can't stay here. We have to go before one of them finds us. Jack said Walter has a gun."

"He does," Jack said.

Kobe kept walking, his steps hesitant. "I need my phone." He didn't want any of them to learn where he lived. "And some light so I can cut these laces. Are you still with us, Jack?"

"Yeah."

"Can you go ahead and check where they are?" Kobe glanced around. Either they were getting closer to one of the lights that were scattered throughout the school grounds or he was becoming accustomed to the dark.

"You're out of your tree. This won't end well."

The only reason Kobe knew Jack was going ahead of them, was due to the direction his voice came from. The ghost made no sound. "Thanks, Jack." He ignored the muttered comments.

"Do you think we're dead?" Xavier's voice came from Kobe's left.

"I don't think so." The cut from the shard of glass stung too much for that.

"Then what? Ghosts aren't real."

"Obviously they are." It was a lot better than thinking they were dead.

Xavier remained silent for a moment as the area continued to lighten, the spotlight visible through the trees. "We could head out the front gate."

"Not without my phone."

"You can get another one."

"I don't care about the phone. I care about them getting my personal information from it." He stopped when there was enough light to see the laces reasonably well. "Hold out your hands and I'll cut through the laces."

"We don't have time for this." Xavier held out his hands, continually scanning the area.

"We'll be able to run faster without our hands tied together." It was easier cutting the shoelaces than it had been cutting the rope. "And laces back in our sneakers."

Xavier stared at Kobe's hands. "How bad are you cut?"

Kobe grinned. "Remember that nose bleed you had earlier this year?"

"The one you gave me?"

"You should have caught the ball with your hands, not your face."

Xavier's smile briefly appeared. "The problem was that you can't throw a ball."

The laces gave way and Kobe held out the shard of glass to Xavier. "No bruise, barely hurt, but it bled for ages."

Xavier took the shard and sawed against the laces when Kobe held out his hands. "So, hardly a scratch."

"Exactly. It's already stopped bleeding."

The laces broke, falling to the ground. Kobe crouched, threading the laces through the top few holes of his sneakers and tying them. He saw that Xavier did the same.

Jack came out of the shadows. "Run. Walter is coming."

"Where are the other two?" Kobe glanced around, unable to see anyone.

"It's safe near the athletics shed, but don't go near the cricket nets," Jack said.

With a nod, Kobe grabbed Xavier's upper arm, tugging him in the direction they needed to go. The moment his friend was moving, he let go, keeping to the outer edges of the buildings, both glad there was limited light and wishing there was more so he could clearly see where he was going. He stumbled on a rock, hearing the pound of footsteps behind him. It had to be Xavier. Leaving the buildings behind, he ran past the different sporting fields, avoiding the light cast from the various spotlights that lit up the fields. He felt exposed, relieved when he was rounding the netball courts that didn't seem to have any lights shining on them.

The distance between him and the footsteps seemed to be growing, but he couldn't bring himself to slow. Xavier would catch up to him when he stopped to look for his phone. Ahead he could see the shadows of the athletics shed, behind him the footsteps were further away. He heard the sound of something colliding, the footsteps no longer following him as he reached the wall of the shed, pressing himself against it.

He forced away the urge to call out to Xavier, peering into the dark, his heart pounding, his breath coming fast. There was silence. "Jack?" He kept his voice soft. "Are you there, Jack?"

"Walter has your friend."

Chapter Seven

Kobe

Kobe nearly jumped at how close Jack's voice was. "Is…" He swallowed hard. "Is he alive?"

"For now."

He had no idea what to do. "Help me find my phone."

"Kobe!"

A shudder ran through him at hearing his name called by the harsh voice. Xavier must have given Walter his name. Crouching low to make it harder for Walter to see him, he moved in the direction Jack gave.

"You have to the count of five before I shoot your friend."

Kobe's hand closed over his phone. There wasn't

time to ring anyone. Or send a text. It'd take too long to turn his phone on.

"One, two."

"What are you doing?" Jack demanded.

Remaining in a crouch, Kobe returned to the shed, jumping up to drop the phone on the roof. He didn't want to risk anyone else taking it from him.

"Three, four."

Kobe straightened, walking towards the voice. "Where are you? I can't see anything in the dark."

"He'll kill the both of you," Jack warned.

"What do you expect me to do?" He kept his voice as low as possible. "Save myself and let Xavier be killed?"

Jack sighed. "No. There has to be something else we can do."

"You better move faster or I'm going to shoot your friend," Walter warned.

"It's dark. I can't see." Kobe lowered his voice, walking faster. "How do you normally help?"

"That didn't stop you from running before. Now move it," Walter ordered.

"It's always different. Mostly by offering advice," Jack said. "A pity none of you ever listen."

They were too close to Walter for Kobe to ask the question that occurred to him. Had all the ones

Jack had previously helped lived? He stopped in front of the shadowy figure of Walter, Xavier kneeling in front of him, hands pressed against the back of his head.

"On the ground," Walter ordered.

Kobe knelt beside Xavier, his back to Walter, like his friend.

"Hands where I can see them," Walter said.

Kobe pressed his hands against the back of his head, trying not to think about the gun Walter held. He kept his gaze on the shadowy figure of Jack, who stood in front of them. He wanted to ask the ghost what they could do, but Walter was behind him and would hear every word.

"One of you are going to find out where Al is for me. I owe him a bullet for trying to kill me. Which one is it going to be? You?"

Kobe felt the gun momentarily pressed against his head, just above where his hands were.

"Or you?"

Kobe barely managed not to turn to see if Walter pressed the gun against Xavier's head. "You go."

"No, I won't–"

Walter interrupted Xavier. "Better make up your mind quick. If they find us I'm shooting you two first."

"I'll stay with you, Walter," Kobe said softly.

"How do you know my name?" Walter pressed the gun against Kobe's head.

Kobe froze. "Alvin told us."

"He had no right." The words were filled with anger. "Start moving, boy."

"Go on, Xavier. I'll be okay." Kobe fought the urge to look towards his friend, keeping his gaze on Jack.

Xavier rose to his feet. "You can have Clara."

A sound escaped Kobe that could almost have been a laugh. "I don't think it works like that. You can't give a person to somebody, Xave."

"Move. Now!" Walter took a step towards Xavier.

Kobe tensed, wanting to tackle Walter to the ground. But he couldn't risk it. This wasn't a game of footy and that wasn't really his sport. Now if he had his cricket bat, it might have been a little different. "Go with him, Jack."

"Who is Jack?" Walter demanded.

"His imaginary friend," Xavier said. "He talks to him when he's stressed. You should hear the kids, at school, pick on him about it." Xavier faced Kobe. "You keep Jack with you. I think you need him more than I do." He took a step backwards.

Kobe shook his head. "Take him with you. He can look out for Alvin and Declan."

"I don't care who has the imaginary friend, but someone better find out where Al is or I'm going to start putting bullets in one of you." Walter pressed the gun against the side of Kobe's head.

"Go," Kobe said softly. "Both of you go."

"Don't go getting yourself shot," Jack warned.

"I'll try not to," Kobe said.

"Who are you talking to?" Walter pressed the gun harder against Kobe's head.

"Jack, of course," Kobe said.

Walter made a noise of disgust before pointing the gun at Xavier, having taken a couple of steps forward so that he stood beside Kobe. "You have ten minutes. Take too long and I'll shoot your friend in the foot. For starters."

"Go," Kobe urged Xavier. He didn't want to be shot.

"Come on." Jack gave Xavier a push in the correct direction. "They shouldn't be too far from where I last saw them."

"Ten minutes," Walter called out. "And time has already started counting down."

Kobe watched the two shadowy figures hurry away, disappearing into the darkness, feeling like he was being deserted. He tried to remind himself he'd told them to go. But the feeling persisted.

"On your feet," Walter ordered. "We're too exposed here."

"You're the only one with a gun," Kobe said. "Staying here means you can see them coming."

"Doesn't mean they don't have one by now. Al might have got his gun out of the car."

Dread pooled in his stomach and he began to regret sending Xavier to find Alvin. "What were you and Alvin fighting about?"

"None of your business." Walter pushed against Kobe's shoulder. "Move."

"Where too?"

"One of the buildings."

"They're locked and have alarms." Kobe winced when Walter grabbed hold of his shoulder and dragged him back, his fingers biting into flesh.

"You better figure something out. If Al comes for me, you go down first."

Fear froze him to the spot, his mind momentarily blank. "The area between the building overlooking the cricket field. It's sheltered on three sides by a 'U' shaped building."

"Lead the way." Walter gave him a shove forward.

Chapter Eight

Kobe

Kobe fought the urge to rub his shoulder where Walter had gripped it. "What about Xavier? Shouldn't we wait and find out where Alvin is first? We have to go past the cricket field to get there."

"You trying to get me killed?" Walter jabbed the gun in Kobe's back.

He stumbled forward, breathing in sharply. "No. But how will you find out what Xavier learns if you go somewhere else? He won't be able to find us."

"Move." Again Walter jabbed him with the gun.

He was torn. What if Alvin had collected his gun? He took several steps forward. But Walter might actually use his gun. Another couple of steps. "We could go around the athletics shed and get a look at the area between there and the classrooms we're heading towards."

"Hurry up then."

It was also the direction Xavier had taken so it might be the way he'd use to return. "This way." He kept his pace slow, scanning the area for movement. He saw nothing, other than the occasional car going past on the nearby road, their lights visible through the tree line. A glance over his shoulder nearly brought him to a stop. "You're bleeding." The blood on Walter's shirt had spread further than the last time he'd seen it.

"You think being stabbed can be fixed with a bandaid?"

Kobe ignored the sarcasm. "You need a doctor."

"What I need is a phone. Al took mine."

"He took mine too." Kobe glanced over his shoulder again. "We can rip your shirt into strips and I can bandage you with them." Maybe he could distract Walter long enough to make a run for it.

"You think you'll be able to do that?" Once again Walter's voice was heavy with sarcasm. "Tear material apart."

The athletics shed came closer and Kobe thought of his phone he didn't dare collect. Not while Walter was with him. "How hard can it be? They do it in the movies all the time."

"If you think life is anything like a movie you're going to be very disappointed."

"I know life isn't like a movie, but some of it's true." He stepped into the shadows of the shed, feeling a little safer. Which was crazy since Walter was behind him with a gun. "You don't want to bleed to death, do you?" He was tempted to let Walter pass out from blood loss, but what would happen to the gun? Would Walter drop it? Fire it? Kill one of them first? He reached the corner of the shed, listening.

"What are you waiting for?"

Before he could speak, he heard a noise. Taking a deep breath, he peered around the corner, freezing when he saw Xavier backing away, his eyes wide.

"Who is it?" Walter demanded.

Words wouldn't form. He watched as Xavier continued to back away, pressed against the shed, almost at the opposite corner. "A toad."

"Then move."

"I'm checking to see if the rest of the area is clear." Where was Jack and why was Xavier at the athletics shed? He was meant to be searching for Alvin and Declan. Not that he wanted his friend to get close to either man.

"Well? How long does it take?"

He spotted Jack striding towards him, clearly visible on the cricket field. Or at least he was visible to him. "I think I see Xavier coming back. We should see what he found out before we cross the cricket field."

"You never said we'd be that exposed." Walter pressed the gun against Kobe's head. "You trying to get me killed?"

Anger rushed through him. "Will you stop doing that?" He instantly froze as he realised what he'd said. "I know you'll shoot me. You don't have to keep reminding me."

Walter pressed the gun more firmly against Kobe's head. "I will remind you as many times as I want." Walter paused a moment. "Got it?"

"Yes." He spoke the word through gritted teeth, his jaw aching with the need to argue.

"How close is your friend?"

Kobe peered around the corner in time to see Jack disappear around the other side of the shed. Him and Xavier came around seconds later, Jack propelling Xavier forward. "He's here."

"What about your imaginary friend? He here too?" Again Walter's tone was filled with sarcasm.

"Yeah, he's here." He drew back as Jack and Xavier

came close, watching as they walked around the corner.

Xavier froze when Walter pointed the gun at him. "They're near the hall." His words tumbled out and he took a step backwards.

"Why are you here?" Jack demanded. "I expected you to be where we left you."

Kobe glanced at Jack, but addressed Xavier. "We're going to the classroom block overlooking the cricket field. Will they see us?"

Xavier shook his head.

Jack was the one to answer. "They're on the other side of the hall. Alvin is sending Declan to get something out of the car. He didn't say what, only that he wanted his gear."

"Move then," Walter said.

Kobe wasn't about to argue. He wanted to be in a safer position before Alvin had his gun. He hurried past the cricket field, Xavier on one side, Jack on the other. "Alvin has a gun in his car."

"Must be what he sent Declan to get." Xavier stumbled. "We're going to end up dead."

"The two of you run the first chance you get," Jack said.

"There's no-" Kobe broke off, unable to finish his argument with Walter behind them. But there was nowhere to go. He had no idea how to break into any of the classrooms. Although that would possibly set off an alarm and have security arriving. Ahead he could see the building they were aiming for.

"Where are you going? I doubt he'd fall for breaking into a classroom," Jack said. "Probably a bad idea anyway. The security guards turn up expecting kids, not men with guns."

He wanted to tell Jack to be quiet. He didn't need any more bad news.

"How far?" Walter demanded.

Kobe glanced over his shoulder and had to stop himself from taking a second look at Walter. The man didn't look too good. "That building over there." He pointed towards it. "It has only one entrance to the central area."

"Are you out of your tree?" Jack demanded. "You'll be pinned in there like chickens in a cage, ready to be slaughtered."

Kobe slowed at Jack's words, glancing towards Xavier who looked over at the same time. He saw the fear on his friend's face, guessing he wore the same expression. "Maybe we should find somewhere else to hide."

"No. Keep moving. We only have to stay low until midnight. And stay up this end."

Kobe wanted to ask Walter what would happen at midnight. But he doubted Walter would tell him and he doubted he really wanted to know. He was struggling to keep going with everything he'd already faced.

"Ask him what happens at midnight," Jack ordered.

Kobe remained silent.

"One of you needs to ask. We need to know what we're in for," Jack said.

Kobe continued to remain silent. Walter wouldn't tell him and asking would only annoy Walter and give him something else to worry about.

"What happens at midnight?" Xavier asked.

"Why are you asking?" Walter demanded. "What do you know?

Kobe nearly groaned. He sent a glare towards Jack, hoping he saw it. Was he trying to get them killed? "Neither of us wants to get killed. Should we be worried about midnight?"

"Do as you're told and you won't get hurt." Walter chuckled. "Or at least not from me." Walter grabbed Kobe by the shoulder as they reached the building. "You go in there and check it's safe. Your friend can stay with me."

Chapter Nine

Kobe wanted to protest. It was dark. He couldn't see a thing. Anything could be in the area between the classrooms. When Walter let him go, he cautiously walked forward. What had made him think this was a good location to hide? He was obviously losing his mind. Being able to see Jack was proof he was losing it.

Jack strode ahead. "There's no one in here."

He started to ask Jack a question, closing his mouth rather than drawing Walter's attention. It took him a few seconds to realise he wasn't afraid. At least not as afraid as he'd been earlier. Was it possible to become so scared that you stopped being scared? Or was it that he expected to die and had accepted the fact? Not that he wanted to die, but he couldn't see any way out of the situation. Reaching the classroom at the far end of the area, he leaned his forehead against the wall. "We're dead, aren't we?"

"No. The angel sent me so you'd have a chance to survive."

He turned so that he was looking towards Jack, his back against the wall. It was too dark to see anything other than shadows. "But you don't know for sure that we'll live through the night."

"No one knows anything for sure."

Kobe pushed away from the wall. "I have to go back to Walter before he shoots Xavier."

"If I cause a distraction will you run?"

"What kind of distraction?"

"I can make a classroom door fly open."

Kobe shook his head. "No. You'll have security guards here and someone is sure to get killed. We need the police."

"I'm the reason the alarms don't always work." There was humour in Jack's voice.

"I'll think about it." He took a couple of steps forward. "Maybe we need a code word or something." A wry smile formed.

"Just twitchin. You're life is in jeopardy and you think it's funny."

There was no point explaining he didn't think it was funny. "Twitchin?"

"Parents used to be a little less lenient about swear words back in my day."

"That'll be the code word." Taking a deep breath he strode towards where he'd left Xavier, finding it easier to walk across ground he'd already travelled.

"Who is it?" Walter demanded.

"Only me. It's safe. I searched every centimetre."

Walter grabbed hold of Kobe's shoulder. "You stay with me. Your mate can watch the entrance. If he runs, you die. Got it?"

"Yes." Xavier's reply was hesitant.

Kobe wanted to demand that Xavier sound a little more confident in his ability to remain on watch. He didn't want to be killed. The shadowy figure of Walter drew him further towards the back of the area. "If you've got a torch I can check your wound for you."

"No."

He had no idea which question Walter answered, but didn't bother asking for clarification. Walter's tone hadn't encouraged talking. He stumbled when Walter did, the man's fingers digging into his shoulder. There was likely to be a bruise at this rate. Midnight couldn't come soon enough. Midnight and finding out if they'd survive the night. "What's the time?"

"How would I know?"

"What do you mean? Don't you have a watch?"

"Al has my phone. I already told you that. Now stop talking and keep walking."

He nearly argued that he hadn't stopped walking. His mouth momentarily dropped open. "How will you know when it's midnight?"

Walter came to a sudden stop. "How-"

Silence stretched out. Kobe remained still, not wanting to do anything to draw Walter's attention. His question had obviously been a bad idea.

"Xavier sent me back to ask if he should get his phone and ring the cops."

Kobe almost jerked in surprise at hearing Jack's voice beside him, barely managing to stay still. How was he meant to answer Jack when Walter stood right next to him?

"Xavier's worried that the two of you will be caught between Walter and Alvin. And whoever else is due here at midnight," Jack said.

Kobe slowly shook his head hoping Walter didn't notice the movement. Somehow he had to figure out what was going on. He wasn't about to stand around and wait to die. "What did Alvin do with your phone? Maybe we can get it."

"We."

Kobe wasn't sure what Walter's tone meant, but it hadn't sounded good.

"Careful," Jack warned.

"Yes, we. You have the two of us. Neither of us can run without risking the other one dying. So, it's we. I want to survive the night and I'm going to do whatever it takes," Kobe said firmly. He was surprised to realise he meant it.

"You should be glad you can't see his expression. Be very careful, Kobe. He's planning something that'll likely get you killed."

"We." Walter's grip loosened.

Kobe wanted to run at what he heard in Walter's voice. It made him think of sharks coming in for the kill. Trying to keep the fear out of his voice, he nodded, even though Walter couldn't see him. "Yes. What do we need to do?"

"You're not going to expect any of the money, are you?" Walter demanded.

"All I want is for me and Xavier to survive the night. And no one to come after us. Then I want to go home and forget this ever happened."

"And your friend? Is he as practical as you?" Walter asked.

"Xavier will do what I tell him."

"I better go warn him," Jack said. "I've got a feeling he's likely to disagree with that statement."

Kobe waited for Walter to speak. The silence stretched out.

"How about we see what your mate has to say." Walter pushed Kobe back towards where they'd come from.

Kobe stumbled beside Walter, hearing Jack warn Xavier to be quiet as they reached him. "Xave, that you?"

"Yeah. What's happening?" Xavier asked.

Kobe was tempted to kick his friend. He was sounding a little too unconcerned. "If we help Walter, he'll let us go home unharmed."

"Okay," Xavier said.

"That's it? Okay? No questions?" Walter sounded suspicious.

"No questions," Xavier said. "I'm sure Kobe's got it all figured out. I trust him. He's my best friend."

Kobe managed not to speak. It was difficult. He wanted to ask why Xavier hadn't trusted him about Clara if he was his best friend.

Walter remained silent.

Chapter Ten

Kobe

It felt like minutes passed, but Kobe was sure it was less than a minute. He forced himself to remain still. If this was a test, he wasn't about to fail it. He stared in the direction he'd heard Xavier's voice, hoping Jack stood beside him and mouthed the words 'stay still'.

"Don't move, Xavier. Walter's thinking. He's not completely convinced. He keeps looking from one to the other even though he can't see either of you," Jack said.

The silence dragged out longer before Walter spoke. "It's all about information. Isn't it always these days?"

"Huh?" Xavier sounded confused.

"How are you meant to get the information from Alvin? And what sort of information?" Kobe asked.

"Bank accounts and passwords. Worth two million dollars to the right buyer." Walter paused a moment. "It's on a USB stick."

Xavier whistled softly. "Do we get a cut of that?"

"Don't be greedy, Xavier." Kobe spoke sharply, hoping his friend wasn't serious.

"Only kidding. But that's a lot of money. Who has that kind of money?"

"Two people are willing to pay that amount for the information. They have the people who can use it without having it traced back to them," Walter said. "If Al hands the information over to his contact I'll get two percent. If I hand it over to my contact, I'll get fifteen percent. Guess who I plan to give it to."

"I'm guessing Alvin is no longer interested in giving you your two percent," Kobe said.

Walter chuckled. "I guess not."

"Why can't you keep the full two million?" Xavier asked.

"Others need to be paid. Ones with the resources to make sure I won't live long enough to spend the money if I try and cut them out." Walter paused a moment. "Someone needs to get that USB stick from Al."

"How are we meant to do that?" Xavier demanded. "We don't know where it is."

"It's in the right pocket of Alvin's jacket. I've seen him take it out a few times and look at it," Jack said.

Kobe repeated Jack's words.

"How do I know you're telling the truth?" Walter demanded.

"Tell Walter it's red," Jack said.

Kobe took a slow, deep breath before he answered. "It's red."

Walter remained silent for a moment. "Think you can get it?"

Kobe didn't hesitate. "Yes."

"Are you crazy?" Xavier demanded.

"He's completely out of his tree," Jack muttered.

Kobe smiled. "No. Not at all. I can do it." As long as Walter believed him, that was all that mattered. He needed time. Without Walter suspecting a thing.

"I'm not staying here," Xavier said. "Alvin's likely to kill you and then Walter will kill me."

Kobe slowly shook his head, mouthing the words 'other plan'. "Of course he won't."

"He's got another plan, you ditz," Jack said.

"I'm not–"

Kobe interrupted Xavier, worried he was about to argue with Jack and remind Walter about his imaginary friend. "I'll look for them at the hall, where Xavier saw them last. I'll wait until Alvin takes the

USB out of his pocket again before I make a grab for it."

"Don't take too long." Walter's grip tightened on Kobe's shoulder before he let him go. "My contact expects it before midnight. He leaves then. He'll be parked on the road south of the cricket field. Alvin's contact is coming in from west of the cricket field."

"You can count on me." Kobe smiled. Yeah, Walter could count on him to get him caught.

"If I can't, both of you will be in body bags before morning," Walter warned.

"That won't need to happen." Kobe walked away, wishing he could tell Jack to follow him. He jumped when Jack spoke from beside him.

"You better have a plan."

Kobe waited until he was further away before he spoke. "I need you to find out where Alvin and Declan are. I'm getting the phones off the roof. Tell Xavier that I've got a plan to get us out of this mess and be ready to run when you tell him."

"Don't be over confident," Jack warned.

A wry smile formed as he glanced towards Jack, enough light in the area that he could barely see him. "It's not confidence. It's desperation. I don't want to die. Or get my friend killed."

Jack nodded. "I'll find you when I figure out where they are."

Kobe's steps slowed as he turned to watch Jack walk away. He felt very alone. A shiver ran through him. Alone and exposed. He broke into a run, heading towards the athletics shed, scanning the area. He needed to know what the time was. If it was close to midnight they wouldn't survive.

Reaching the shed, he pressed himself against it as he listened. The area was silent. There were the usual night noises. Insects, cars going past, dogs barking in the distance, bursts of music from some of the cars. But nothing out of the ordinary and nothing nearby. He walked around to the other side of the shed, remaining in the shadows, before he jumped for the guttering and pulled himself onto the roof.

Crouching low, he glanced around the area. No one was nearby. Up on the roof there was enough light to see the two phones against the light colour of the corrugated metal sheeting. He collected his phone on the way to Xavier's, pressing the power button. He slipped it into his pocket while he waited for it to turn on.

Xavier's phone had stopped recording, reaching it's size limit and saving the file. He was tempted to view it, but there wasn't time. He needed to call the police and let them know what was happening. Checking his phone, he saw it was still turning on. He'd use Xavier's phone. Before he could, a sound had him pressing himself against the cold metal of the roof and inching towards the edge to peer over.

Alvin slapped Declan on the side of the head as they walked towards the athletics shed. "We can't leave, you idiot. Anyway, Walter's probably bled to death by now. I know I got him good."

"But what if he's alive? He'll shoot us when we go out there to give them the information." Declan motioned towards the cricket field.

Declan's words reminded Kobe he hadn't checked the time. He'd been too focused on calling the police. He pressed a button at the side of Xavier's phone and the screen lit up. His heart felt like it stopped. There was an hour and forty-five minutes left. Not enough time. Nowhere near enough time.

"I'll keep an eye out for Walter while you make the exchange." Alvin patted Declan on the back. "It's not like he has a sniper. I'll shoot him before he can point his gun at you." With his other hand, Alvin raised his gun and mimed shooting someone.

"But-"

Alvin interrupted Declan. "You're like the son I

never had. Do you think I'd let anything happen to you?"

Chapter Eleven

Kobe nearly shook his head, stopping himself at the last second, worried the movement would catch their attention. It was probably a good thing Alvin had never had a son. His phone beeped to let him know of missed messages and he drew back, lying flat as he tried to take the phone from the pocket he'd shoved it in.

"What was that noise?" Declan asked.

Kobe held in the button to turn off his phone, doing the same to Xavier's, not wanting to risk taking the time to set them to silent. Someone might ring.

"Look around. Sounded like a phone. Did you turn off the one you took from the kid before you threw it away?" Alvin demanded.

"Of course I did." Declan was quiet a moment. "At

least I think so." Another pause. "It was different to mine. Maybe it doesn't work the same."

Kobe held his breath, remaining pressed against the roof, hearing what sounded like Alvin hitting Declan again, calling him an idiot. Both the phones were off. He closed his eyes, not knowing what to do. He was stuck on the roof until Alvin and Declan left the area.

"Bet you didn't expect this to happen."

Kobe opened his eyes to find Jack standing over him. He didn't dare answer the ghost.

"I gave your message to Xavier. He wasn't able to speak. Walter was standing right next to him with the gun pressed against his head. Seems like Xavier made a comment that Walter didn't like, judging by what he was saying.

Kobe momentarily closed his eyes again, sighing softly. When would Xavier learn? He stared up at Jack, wishing he could ask him if he had any suggestions. Time was running out. Quicker than he'd expected. He'd thought they had a couple of hours left when he'd made the agreement with Walter.

"Find the phone and stop shining the light everywhere." Alvin's tone was terse, his footsteps heavy as he strode away.

"You're going to have to throw your phone down

there," Jack said. "I doubt he's going to leave the area before he finds it. You'll have to turn it on too."

He was about to say he couldn't do that, when he realised he could. Everything was on the SIM and SD cards in his phone. Removing the back cover and battery, he took both the cards out and slipped them into a pocket of his jeans before putting the phone back together and turning it on.

Kobe sat up slightly to look for Declan.

Jack pressed him back against the roof. "Do you want to get caught?"

"He's going to hear me throw the phone down there."

Jack started to speak, smiling instead. "What was the excuse you gave before? Toad. There's sure to be at least one of them around here. Throw your phone near one and it'll not only catch Declan's attention, but give him a reason for the noise."

"How am I meant to find one from up here?"

"Stay low and I'll find one. When I raise my hand there'll be a toad directly in front of my feet." Jack swung off the roof before Kobe could argue.

He inched over to the side of the roof. It sounded like a terrible plan. How was he meant to throw while lying down? He saw Jack raise his hand. It looked like he had little choice. A glance at Declan showed he had his back to Jack. The timing wasn't about to get any better. He tossed the phone at Jack's feet, ducking back at the noise.

"Who's there?" Declan demanded. He laughed nervously. "Toads." His voice was filled with disgust.

Kobe watched as the beam of light from the torch paused on the phone lying in the grass. Declan remained still for a moment before he walked towards it and picked it up. Kobe held his breath as Declan shined the torch around the area again.

"Thought I'd checked over here. Guess the toad was on it." He strode towards the toad, kicking out at it. The creature was too quick, jumping towards the trees.

Jack joined Kobe on the roof. "Want me to follow them and see what they plan to do?"

He hesitated. There wasn't much time left and he hadn't been able to make a call. "Okay. Fifteen minutes at the most. We need to get Xavier before Walter thinks I'm not coming back."

Jack nodded before jumping off the roof, striding after Declan.

Kobe watched him leave as he turned on Xavier's phone. If his friend had changed his pin then he wasn't going to be able to ring anyone other than emergency. But that would do. He didn't need to ring anyone else. The problem would be that he wouldn't be able to change the settings to silent. The moment the phone was on, he put in the pin, relieved it worked. Going to the settings he turned off all sounds, not wanting to risk being caught out again. He noticed there were missed calls and messages from both his mum and Xavier's mum. For a second the thought of facing Walter paled compared to facing his mum and telling her what they'd done.

He hadn't gone straight to Xavier's house. Bringing up the keypad, he stared at the phone. What could he say to the police? Would they believe him? Fear raced through him, causing his heart to beat at a ridiculous rate. What if no one came to help them?

The screen darkened, timing out. About to press the button to access the screen again, he nearly dropped it when the phone screen lit up by itself. It took him a couple of seconds to realise it was an incoming call. His mum was ringing. Relief rushed through him. She would believe him. His mum would believe him if he told her he was in trouble. And she wouldn't yell at him. At least not until he was home safely. The call ended and he started to dial 000. If the police didn't believe him, then he'd call his mum. Get her to convince them.

Jack joined him on the roof. "They're searching the

area near the main gates, working their way around towards Xavier and Walter. At the speed they're going we've got about twenty to thirty minutes." He nodded to the phone. "Have you rung yet?"

He checked the time. It was ten-forty. He'd have to ring the police after they rescued Xavier. It'd probably take too long to tell them everything. And he wasn't about to let Walter shoot Xavier. His friend trusted him to return.

"I'll do it later." Kobe shoved the phone in his pocket. "Think you can open the athletics shed for me?"

"I can, but how will that help?"

Kobe swung over the side of the roof, dropping to the ground. "I'm not about to return to Walter empty handed."

Jack walked through the door of the shed twice before it swung open. "What are you looking for?"

He thought for a moment. It had only been a couple of days since he'd been in the shed. A smile slowly formed. "Tennis net and cricket bat."

"Interesting combination." Jack showed Kobe where the items were.

Kobe hoisted the net onto his left shoulder and held the bat in his right hand. "Go ahead of me and check where Walter is." He'd leave the net at the side of the building. He wanted both hands on the bat when he went after Walter.

Jack returned before Kobe reached the classroom block. "They're in the same place, give or take a few inches.

"Does Walter have the gun pointed at Xavier's head?"

"Yeah." Jack was silent a moment. "What do you want to do?

"Not get either of us killed." He placed the net at the side of the building, remaining there as he tried to figure out how to manage that. "On which side of Xavier is Walter standing?"

"The side closest to us."

"I'm going around the building to the other side. When I let them know I'm back, make one of the classroom doors on this side of the building slam open. Keep opening them until he's distracted."

"What do you plan to do?"

It took him a few seconds to think of how to get Xavier out of the way. He smiled, one that didn't feel in the slightest bit pleasant. "Not get either of us killed." His grip tightened on the bat. "Tell Xavier to remember the bowling ball game." He strode away, ignoring Jack's question as to what that meant.

The back of the building wasn't as dark as the

other side and he couldn't help glancing around, half expecting someone to jump out and grab him. Xavier better remember the bowling ball game. He'd complained enough about the console game they'd spent months playing last year. The character Xavier had chosen meant he spent most of his time rolling out of the way instead of attacking, feeling like he was a bowling ball. The name had stuck for the game. He walked along the side of the 'U' shaped building. This was crazy. He was about to take on a gun wielding lunatic with a cricket bat.

Chapter Twelve

Kobe

Reaching the opening of the 'U' Kobe paused, taking a deep breath. How was he meant to find them?

"Over here," Jack called out.

Relief rushed through Kobe. What would they have done without Jack? And what had he done to deserve his help? He didn't believe in angels so why would one send someone to help him? Pushing aside those thoughts, he strode towards where he'd heard Jack's voice. "Walter? Where are you?" He kept his voice low.

"You get it?" Walter demanded.

"Of course I did." His steps slowed. When was Jack going to cause a distraction?

"Blast it. The door isn't opening," Jack said.

"Give it here," Walter said.

"I can't see you." Kobe stopped walking. Walter had sounded too close.

A bang made Kobe jump. For a second he thought it was the gun, then realised it was a door.

"Who's there?" Walter demanded.

"The gun is pointed at me," Jack said.

Kobe raised the bat. "Bowling ball." Squeezing his eyes closed, hoping that Xavier was out of the way, he swung. The impact jarred through his arms and he drew the bat back again at Walter's bellow. "Jack, show Xavier where the net is." He swung once more, lower this time, the impact drowning out the sound of Xavier running towards the net.

Walter screamed. "Wait until I get-"

Kobe swung once more.

"Step back, Kobe," Jack ordered. "Xavier has the net."

Kobe backed away.

"What the-" Walter began. He gasped.

"What's happening?" Kobe demanded.

Jack chuckled. "Xavier landed on him. You might want to give him a hand before he gets tangled in the net."

Kobe worried about how long it took to tie Walter up with the net, gagging him with his own shirt since it was impossible to remove Walter's. He helped

Xavier shove him in the open classroom in a spot where Walter wouldn't be seen from a window. He put on his hoodie, zipping it up halfway. "Where's the gun?"

"I've got it," Xavier said.

"Get rid of it. We have no idea how to use one and are likely to get ourselves killed," Kobe said.

"No. I'm not going to let anyone hold a gun to my head. You weren't the one standing here worried Walter might shoot you."

"Alvin and Declan are getting close," Jack warned.

"Can you lock the door?" Kobe gestured towards the classroom they'd shoved Walter in.

"Yeah." A minute later Jack spoke again. "It's done."

"Can you unlock another classroom?" Kobe had to make sure Xavier didn't get either of them killed with the gun he'd taken from Walter. They needed to get away from the building before Alvin found them. They could probably get away from Declan, but not Alvin. Especially since he now carried a gun.

"It's open," Jack said.

"We're not hiding here, are we?" Xavier asked.

Kobe moved closer to where he'd heard Xavier's voice. "Does the gun have a safety? At least use it so you don't shoot yourself. Or me."

"I don't know. How am I meant to know what one looks like?" Xavier asked.

"Let me see." He took the gun Xavier gave him, trying to move towards where he'd heard Jack, without making a sound.

"What are you doing?" Xavier's voice was filled with suspicion.

Kobe found the open door and slipped the gun inside on the floor against the wall, pulling the door shut. "Lock it, Jack."

Jack chuckled. "You know he's not going to trust you again after that."

"What did you do?" Xavier demanded. "Where's my gun?"

"Locked away." Kobe moved closer to Xavier. "Where's the cricket bat, Jack?"

"About two feet to your right," Jack said.

"You do know we mostly use metres now." Kobe stumbled over the bat.

"Not me. I'll see where Alvin is. Head to the groundsman's shed."

"Why there?" Kobe waited for Jack to answer.

"I think he's already gone," Xavier said.

Kobe drew in a deep breath, checking the time on Xavier's phone. They had fifty-five minutes left. It hadn't taken as long to overpower Walter as he'd feared. "Come on." He put the phone back in his pocket.

"Is that my phone?" Xavier walked beside Kobe.

"I haven't managed to ring anyone yet and Declan has my phone."

"What happened?"

"I'll tell you later." Kobe glanced around the area, disliking how much light was in this part of the school grounds. "Race you to the groundsman's shed." He broke into a run. Behind him he heard Xavier's footsteps. Remembering last time they'd made a run for it, he slowed so his friend could come alongside him.

"Why would Jack send us to the groundsman's shed?"

"I don't know." They entered a shadowy area and Kobe felt safer. "He better have a good reason."

"Because I've got a space in the back of the shed where you can hide."

"Will you stop doing that?" Xavier demanded. "Like I haven't had enough scares tonight."

Kobe had to agree with Xavier. "Can't you make a noise?"

"Yeah, rattle some chains or something," Xavier muttered.

"I don't have any chains. All I have is what I died with."

"Oh."

Kobe smiled at how uncomfortable Xavier had sounded. He slowed as they approached the groundsman's shed, the building a darker shadow amongst the trees. He took out the phone, using the light of the screen to see better. He didn't dare use the flashlight app. Anyone could be in the area. They didn't need to run into anyone else tonight.

"Why didn't we use that earlier?" Xavier asked.

"Because we didn't want Alvin to see us." He checked the time as they entered the shed. Forty-five minutes. There wasn't much time left.

"This way." Jack led the way to an area behind a wardrobe, walking through it.

"How are we meant to fit through that gap?" Xavier stopped in front of the wardrobe, eyeing the gap between the side of it and the wall.

Kobe grinned, lightly hitting his friend's lean stomach with the back of his hand. "Shouldn't eat so much junk food."

"Ha, ha, very funny," Xavier muttered.

Chapter Thirteen

Kobe

Kobe pushed past his friend and entered the space sideways, his back pressed against the wall. It wasn't as tight a fit as he'd first thought. He shined the light, from the phone, over the area behind the wardrobe. There was a brown cushion on the floor, a battery-powered lantern beside it and a photocopy of a blond haired, blue eyed girl, on the wall. "Who is that?" Kobe nodded towards the picture.

"Rose." Jack gestured towards the cushion. "I'm afraid I've only got one, but this is the first time I've had to help two at the same time. Only the ones I help can see me."

Xavier squeezed into the area. "Lucky. Or one of us would have thought the other had gone crazy." He turned on the lantern. "You can't imagine how sick I am of the dark."

Remaining standing, Kobe dialled emergency.

Xavier sat on the cushion. "Where did this stuff come from?" He gestured towards the lantern.

"Gifts."

"From those you've helped?" Xavier asked.

Kobe half listened to Xavier and Jack talk as he explained his emergency, frequently checking the time. It was rapidly disappearing. "You need to hurry," Kobe said, when the operator continued to ask him questions.

"Officers have been dispatched. But every bit of information you can give us will help."

"There isn't anything else I can tell you." He checked the time. Thirty minutes. "How far away are they?"

"They are on their way. Are you in a safe location?"

Kobe felt like growling in frustration. He rested the bat against the back wall in case he was tempted to use it. "How would I know? I wouldn't have a clue where Alvin and Declan are. I've already told you that."

Jack and Xavier fell silent, both looking at Kobe.

He took a deep breath. "Sorry, I-" He had no idea what to say.

"Remain calm. You said you have a friend with you. Would he be able to give us further details?"

"I don't know. Maybe. Hang on." Kobe held the phone out to Xavier. "She wants to talk to you."

"What for?" Xavier rose to his feet, taking the phone.

Kobe shrugged. "I don't know. In case you know more than me, I guess."

Xavier pressed the phone to his ear. "Hello?" His voice was hesitant.

Kobe looked around the small space, made smaller with the three of them in it. His gaze was drawn to the cricket bat, noticing blood on the timber. "You don't think Walter will die, do you?"

Jack shrugged. "He didn't look too good before you hit him. But if he dies, it won't be from what you did. It'll be from Alvin stabbing him." Jack's gaze was drawn back to the bat. "I used to play with my mates. Not after my mum died, but before." He paused a moment, his eyes unfocused. "Before everything fell apart."

Kobe tried to think what to say, hearing Xavier talking in the background. It sounded like he was answering the same questions emergency had already asked him.

"Australia won the Ashes the year I died. I heard

it on the radio. But everything seemed lame to me. I couldn't capture the feeling I had when they won in fifty-nine." Jack shrugged. "I guess not much interested me that year." His gaze was drawn to the picture. "Other than Rose."

"What happened?" Kobe looked at the picture. "Why did you kill her?"

"It was an accident."

Guessing Jack wasn't about to tell him all the details, he decided to ask the question that was bothering him. "Why me? And why Xavier? What did we do to deserve the angel sending you to help us?"

"Nothing. I don't think it works like that. If someone at this school is in trouble, I have to help them so I can atone for my sins. The major and the minor ones."

A wry smile formed and Kobe was tempted to laugh. "I did do something then. I came to this school."

Jack chuckled. "I guess you did. Although that wasn't the case for one of them."

"We're going to be late."

The sound of Declan's voice outside had them falling silent, staring at the back wall.

"What part of don't speak didn't you understand?" Alvin demanded. "I told you I heard voices."

"But-" Declan started to speak.

"I know you're in there." Alvin raised his voice. "Come out or I'll start randomly shooting the shed. You might get lucky and I'll miss. Or..." Alvin chuckled instead of finishing his sentence.

Kobe shared a look with Xavier. They couldn't stay inside. They had to go out there and face Alvin and his gun.

"Actually, stay in there. I like the second option best," Alvin said.

"I'm coming." Kobe checked the time on the phone Xavier held then pointed to the lantern, mouthing the word 'out'. Eleven-forty. Alvin was cutting it close for the meeting with his contact.

"And your mate," Alvin ordered.

"He's not in here. I was trying to figure out what to do." Kobe squeezed between the wall and the wardrobe. "I talk aloud when I'm trying to sort things out."

"I will have a look," Alvin warned.

"You can't see the gap beside the wardrobe clearly from the doorway," Jack said. "He shouldn't be able to see it with only the light from a torch."

Kobe hoped Jack was right. He stumbled when

the lantern went out just before he reached the door. "You can look all you want, but my friend ditched me. Guess he was right that it was safer to run than hide." He opened the door, his breath catching when he saw that Alvin stood outside, the torch light shining on the ground at his feet. But that wasn't what held his attention. Kobe couldn't take his gaze off the gun pointed at his face.

"Step back and to the side." Alvin shined the torch across the contents of the shed the moment Kobe was out of the way. He stepped back. "Get out here and walk towards the cricket field."

Kobe thought of the cricket bat he'd left behind. Not that it would have been a good idea to use it against two opponents. Both who had torches and one who had a gun. "I thought you'd be meeting your friend by now. It's nearly midnight."

"What do you know about that?" Alvin demanded.

"Walter was complaining about it. Said you should have been paying him a bigger share. That you were ripping him off." Kobe kept walking towards the cricket field, having no idea what else he could do.

"Be. Quiet." Alvin emphasised each word.

"I'm never kissing another girl," Kobe muttered.

"The problem was kissing the wrong girl," Jack said.

Kobe glanced to the side, surprised to see Jack nearby. "Technically, I didn't kiss her."

"What are you going on about?" Alvin demanded.

"Him and Xavier were fighting over a girl earlier. One that Kobe had kissed," Declan said.

"Did I ask you?" Alvin demanded.

"Next time find a girl who's interested in the things you like," Jack said. "That way she'll be interested in going to the places you both want to visit."

"I don't think you should be giving me dating advice. Not with your history," Kobe said softly.

"I didn't give you any advice." Declan sounded confused.

"I have to do everything myself." Alvin grabbed Kobe by the shoulder and turned him. "Don't move from here."

Chapter Fourteen

Kobe

There was enough light that Kobe could see Alvin give Declan the gun.

"Hold that on him and shoot him if he moves. I've got about ten minutes to get in place or this deal will fall through." Alvin strode away before Declan could raise the gun.

"What now, Jack?" Kobe asked.

"It's Declan."

Kobe grinned. "I know."

"But you…" Declan's voice trailed off, his eyes narrowing. "Keep talking and I'll shoot. I don't have to take that anymore."

Kobe's grin faded. "I wasn't picking on you, Declan. How would you like it if I pointed a gun at you? That's worse than picking on someone."

"Alvin points a gun at me all the time." Declan shrugged. "He said there's nothing wrong with pointing it at someone, it's pulling the trigger that's the problem."

Kobe tried not to feel any sympathy for Declan, but it was difficult. Pointing a gun at someone was a bad idea. Someone could get shot. "Doesn't make it right just because Alvin says it is." When Declan only shrugged again, he tried a different topic. "Why do you call him Alvin when Walter calls him Al?"

"He doesn't like Al. Walter only calls him Alvin when he doesn't want to annoy him." A sound behind Declan had him looking over his shoulder. "You-"

Spotting Xavier stepping into a less shadowy spot, Kobe tackled Declan to the ground, struggling to keep the man from rising.

"Run. He's lost his gun. It's a good six feet from him," Jack said.

Xavier helped Kobe to his feet. "Come on. This way."

Kobe followed Xavier towards the main entrance of the school. "Why this way?"

"It's nowhere near where Alvin is meeting his contact."

"Don't slow down," Jack warned. "Declan found his gun and is heading towards you."

"This night has been one disaster after another," Kobe muttered.

"I'm sorry," Xavier said.

Kobe glanced towards his friend. "What for?"

"Wanting to make you run around the track. We've been friends long enough I should have known not to listen to Clara."

Kobe frowned. "What do you mean?"

"She said you were the one who kissed her."

"You spoke to her about it?" He'd been teasing when he'd said earlier that Xavier couldn't talk to Clara without stuttering. It wasn't true, but he did tend to stumble over some of his words and struggle to think of what to say to her. "An entire conversation?"

"You can talk about this later," Jack said. "He's getting closer. Run faster."

"I've got a feeling he's had a lot of practice at running and we'd be better off finding somewhere to hide." Kobe glanced over his shoulder, but couldn't see Declan.

"This is probably the worst direction to take for hiding. There's too many lights," Xavier said.

"This way." Kobe veered to the left. "We'll head back towards the building where we left Walter."

"I am not hiding with Walter," Xavier protested.

"You're not going to make it that far," Jack warned. "He'll reach you before then."

"Run faster," Kobe urged.

"I can't. This is it. You go ahead."

Kobe shook his head. He wasn't about to desert Xavier. How could he? Xavier hadn't deserted him. "Open a classroom." He veered to the closest one.

Jack walked through the door and it sprung open.

Kobe winced at the noise. "He'll have heard that."

"I can't always get it to work right. Want me to open the next classroom?"

Kobe nodded, then shook his head. "The one after that." He ran after Jack, Xavier a few steps behind him.

Jack stepped through the door. There was a soft clicking sound. "Try that."

Kobe turned the handle, relief rushing through him when the door swung open. "Hurry." He dragged Xavier into the room with him, closing the door behind them. He crouched low so he couldn't be seen through the windows. "Can you lock it?" For a moment he feared Jack couldn't hear him, but he didn't dare speak any louder. There were noises outside that likely meant Declan was nearby.

Jack stepped through the door several times before there was a soft clicking sound. "That should be locked." He walked through the wall. "He's in the first classroom, looking under desks."

Kobe leaned close to Xavier. "Where's your phone."

Xavier turned his head to whisper in Kobe's ear. "I left it under the wardrobe in case we were caught. I told emergency what had happened and that I was going after you. She told me to remain where I was and that help was on the way."

"Not that I've noticed." Kobe wanted to stand up and see what was happening. He remained pressed against the wall under the window.

"He's coming out of the classroom," Jack said.

"I don't know which would be worse," Xavier whispered. "Not knowing what's happening or Jack's commentary."

"He's checking the handle of the next classroom."

"I think they're as bad as each other." Kobe looked towards the window. Would Declan be able to see them if he looked through it?

"He's shining his torch in each of the windows and doing a visual search of the room," Jack said.

"I think the commentary is worse. How can we get him to stop?" Xavier asked.

Kobe didn't reply when he heard the handle of the classroom door rattle.

"He's at your door," Jack said.

Kobe bit back a sarcastic reply. As if he could have missed that. He held his breath when torchlight ran across the floor, highlighting desks and chairs. He tensed as it came closer.

Jack stepped through the wall to stare down at them. "Don't move. As long as you can see me, you're in danger."

Kobe wanted to speak. There were questions he needed to ask. Seeing Xavier move slightly, he looked towards him, reaching for his friend when he saw him open his mouth. He shook his head. Pressing a finger against his lips, gripping Xavier's shoulder.

"Don't speak," Jack warned. "He's standing right beside you."

Kobe's grip tightened. He loosened it when Xavier winced. His gaze was drawn to the beam of light as it passed them, travelling across the rest of the classroom. Then it was gone and he sagged back against the wall, letting go of Xavier.

"He's still there. Hasn't moved yet," Jack said.

Footsteps sounded outside. A gunshot rang out in

the distance and Kobe froze, his breath catching. The footsteps stopped. Everything remained silent. He turned to look at the window above him.

"Remain down." Jack took several steps to the side. "He's across from me."

Kobe's gaze was drawn along the wall. A metre. Declan was too close. His body ached from remaining still and tense. He wanted to run. Wanted to get out of here before Declan could find them.

The next window along shattered, glass raining onto the floor, Declan climbing through. He froze when he caught sight of the two of them huddled against the wall.

Kobe angled his body so that he was in front of Xavier. There was no need for both of them to be shot and he was the one in the middle.

"Don't make any sudden movements." Jack looked from Kobe to Declan. "He looks more surprised than you. Stay still and remain calm."

"Stop speaking," Xavier snapped. "Just stop. I can't listen anymore."

"Try not to wig out," Jack said.

Kobe momentarily closed his eyes, opening them to see Declan point his gun at them, crouching low.

"No one said anything." Declan tried to look past Kobe, who remained in front of Xavier. "And you better not say anything. We're going to stay here until it's safe to go. I bet that was Walter."

"Want me to see what's going on?" Jack asked.

Chapter Fifteen

Kobe

Kobe looked towards Jack, nodding, catching movement out of the corner of his eye. He turned enough to see Xavier had pressed his hands over his ears. He almost smiled. But it didn't form. His gaze was drawn to Declan when Jack walked through the wall. As Jack had pointed out, they weren't safe if they could see him. Having a gun pointed directly at them certainly wasn't safe.

Declan moved closer, his gun remaining on them. "Walter will shoot you too." He crept closer. "He won't care who you are."

Kobe wasn't tempted to tell him they'd already dealt with Walter. He doubted Walter had managed to escape. Not with how they'd tangled him in the tennis net.

"You hear me?" Declan demanded, keeping his voice low.

"Yeah. We met Walter. We don't want to run into him again," Kobe said.

"When did you meet him?" Declan asked.

"Earlier. He wasn't looking too good. Had lost a lot of blood." Kobe inched backwards, running into Xavier who didn't move.

Declan came closer, glass crunching under his boots. "He's mean when he's hurt. We can't let him find us." Glass crunched as he came closer.

Kobe pressed back against Xavier, wanting to tell his friend to move. "Last time we saw him he was on the far side of the school. And that gunshot didn't sound close."

"He'll look for us. Alvin didn't have a gun. Walter is the only other one with a gun. I don't know what I'd do without Alvin. He's always been there for me. No one else. Only him." Declan moved close enough that the gun was centimetres from Kobe. "Walter will kill me. He threatened to kill me and Alvin. It was Alvin who stopped him."

"He said he'd kill us too." Xavier shifted back slightly. "He held a gun against my head for ages."

Kobe shifted back, trying not to look at the gun that was directly in front of his face.

Declan nodded. "That sounds like Walter." He came closer.

Kobe wanted to tell him to stop moving. Then he realised he could. "You're making too much noise. The glass under your boots. It's really loud when you move."

Declan looked down at his feet, the gun lowering slightly. "I had to break it."

"I know." Kobe had no idea what to do. He pressed back against Xavier who shifted a little more.

Jack walked through the wall. "The fuzz are here. They arrested a man who was in a car south of the cricket field, Walter who they took away in an ambulance, as well as Alvin and his contact who they had to chase. He was the one who fired the gun."

"Where are they?" Xavier asked.

Kobe wanted to tell him to be quiet.

"Where is who?" Declan asked.

"Walter of course," Kobe spoke quickly. "I'll stand up and look out the window to see if he's out there."

"Don't try anything." Declan said.

"If you're asking about the cops, they're searching for the two of you. Found the phone you left under the wardrobe and the cricket bat. Hope you weren't wanting it for a souvenir."

"Do you want me to look?" Kobe kept his gaze on Declan.

"Listen to him," Jack said. "Don't try anything."

What did Jack expect? For them to remain here all night with a gun pointed at them? "What do you say, Declan?"

"A quick look. Don't let him see you."

"Okay. I won't. I don't want him to find us either." Kobe took a deep breath before he rose enough to peer over the edge of the window.

Jack stepped through the wall next to him. "No one is in the area yet. Don't escape until help is nearby. I'd tell you not to try anything, but I've got a feeling I'd be wasting my breath."

Kobe half smiled at Jack's tone. The smile faded before he returned to where he'd been crouching. "There's no one out there. Maybe we should leave before Walter reaches this part of the school." Declan would never let them go if he knew the police were here.

"I'm not going anywhere," Xavier said. "I'm sick of having a gun pointed at me. You can have it pointed at you for a change."

"No one is going anywhere. Not until Walter stops looking for us," Declan said.

Kobe had no idea what to say. He didn't want to

explain that Walter wouldn't be coming after them as that would lead to questions it wouldn't be a good idea to answer. Ones involving a net and a bat. He didn't want Declan any more wary of them than he already was. "What did you do with my phone?"

"What?"

"My phone. I tried to find it where you threw it, but it wasn't there." Kobe had almost forgotten he wasn't meant to know Declan had found it.

"Nice save," Jack said.

Declan took the phone from a pocket of his jacket and held it out to Kobe. "Don't turn it on."

"Thanks." He slipped it into a pocket of his hoodie.

"What happened to your shirt?" Declan gestured towards Kobe's chest, using the gun.

Chapter Sixteen

Kobe

Kobe frantically tried to think of an excuse. Maybe he shouldn't have tried to talk to Declan. But remaining crouched in the classroom with a gun pointed at him while no one spoke had been too uncomfortable. "Walter used it to wrap up his wound."

Declan started to speak, when the glow from the lights outside increased. Remaining crouched against the wall, he looked towards the broken window. "What's going on?"

Kobe had no idea what to tell him. The only way the light could have brightened was if someone had turned extra ones on.

Jack walked through the wall, coming straight back. "It's the cops. Tell him someone must have walked past the light sensor."

Kobe repeated the second half of Jack's information.

Xavier started to rise to his feet. "I'll check who it is."

Declan pointed the gun at Xavier. "Don't move. Walter will see where you came from."

"No he won't," Kobe said. "Not if Xavier moves now. He can't see this section of the building from where he is."

"So I'll go?" Xavier nodded towards the window.

"Give me a chance to think," Declan said. "I need to figure out what to do."

"He doesn't have time to think." Jack remained by the window, looking out from it. "The cop is moving away from the area."

"Declan-" Kobe started to say.

"No. Give me a minute." Declan clutched at the side of his head with one hand while continuing to keep the gun pointed at them with the other.

"You're running out of time," Jack warned.

Kobe wished he could demand a minute to think. Taking a deep breath, he met Jack's gaze. "Twitchin."

"I hope you know what you're doing." Jack walked through the wall.

"What-"

Kobe interrupted Xavier. "Almost like last time. Except without the cricket bat and no rolling."

"What are you planning?" Declan demanded.

The classroom door slammed open as Jack strode through it.

Declan jumped to his feet, pointing the gun at the doorway. "Who's there? What's going on?"

Kobe launched himself at Declan. "Run, Xave. Run!"

The gun was knocked from Declan's hand to skitter across the floor. "No." Declan tried to twist away from Kobe, reaching for the gun.

Kobe heard running footsteps, unable to check if it was Xavier. A shout came from outside and Declan continued to try and escape.

"Don't let him go." Jack knelt beside Kobe. "If you can see me, you aren't safe."

"Do you think I don't know that?" The words burst from Kobe at the same moment as Declan twisted out of his grip. He started to lunge for the man.

"Out the window." Jack dragged Kobe to his feet. "Run."

Kobe jumped out the window, Jack walking through the wall beside him. He saw police running towards the open door, one officer holding Xavier back from returning to the classroom. There was a confusion of noise, gunshots were fired and Jack dragged him to the side.

Kobe started to ask Jack what was happening, but the ghost vanished and he was left lying beside the wall by himself, staring up at an officer who held out a hand to him. Taking it, he allowed the officer to help him to his feet, nodding when he was asked if he was okay.

He slowly turned around. Jack was gone. Apparently he was safe. Him and Xavier. But what about Jack? What would happen to him? He watched as two officers led Declan away in handcuffs.

"Are you certain you're unharmed?" the officer asked again.

Kobe nodded. "I just want to go home." He sighed when the police officer began a spiel that included mention of the police station, statements to be given and questions to be answered. They'd already told emergency everything. He watched as Xavier walked towards him, shaking his head at whatever the accompanying officer was saying. He grinned. More than likely Xavier was being told the same and wanted to go home as much as he did.

"We've got to go to the police station." Xavier stopped in front of Kobe, sending a glare towards the officer who accompanied him.

"I know." He clapped Xavier on the shoulder. "We should probably get it over and done with. But you might want to ring home first. Our mums have left a ridiculous amount of messages."

Xavier looked him up and down. "You okay?"

"Yeah."

"When I heard the gunshots…" Xavier's voice trailed off. "They wouldn't let me go. I tried to come back and help you."

He clapped Xavier on the shoulder again. "It's okay." He took out his phone and pulled off the back, slotting in the cards. "We better ring our mums." He felt strangely shaky.

"Can I borrow your phone? They've taken mine. For evidence."

"Yeah." He put the phone back together.

"Are you ready to go to the police station now?" one of the officers asked.

Kobe's gaze was drawn to where he'd last seen Jack. "There's a lot I couldn't tell you. So much of the night is a blur." He looked down at his phone when it beeped. Twelve thirty-nine. Less time had passed than he'd expected. It had felt like an eternity when they'd been pressed against the wall of the classroom with a gun pointed at them.

"This way." The officer gestured towards the main entrance of the school.

After one more look at where he'd last seen Jack, Kobe slung an arm around Xavier's shoulders as they walked towards the main entrance. "So, about Clara." He flicked through some of the messages from his mum, trying to find the courage to call her. After having a gun pointed at him he would have thought it'd be easier than this.

"Not happening," Xavier said.

"That wasn't what I was about to ask. All forgotten?"

"Yeah." Xavier met Kobe's gaze. "But I'll never forget tonight. You didn't have to come back for me."

He pulled up his mum's number, stopping to face Xavier. "Of course I did, Xave. We're mates. Nothing will ever change that." When Xavier nodded, he smiled, continuing to walk towards the main entrance as he hit the button to call his mum.

Chapter Seventeen

Jack

Jack saw Kobe and Xavier huddled not far from the groundsman's shed, talking softly. Kobe held a cricket bat and Xavier carried a cricket ball. He smiled. It had been over a week since he'd seen them. He'd begun to think they wouldn't return to school before the holidays started at the end of this week. But here they were, before school started for the day and on the last Monday before term ended for a fortnight.

He moved closer, smiling as he listened to them.

"He probably isn't here. It's not like he'd be waiting around for us to come and thank him." Xavier turned the ball in his hand.

Kobe shrugged. "Doesn't matter. The least we can do is thank him in the hope he can hear us."

"What if he's…" Xavier shrugged. "I don't know,

doesn't exist when he's not helping someone. He did vanish."

"Doesn't mean he doesn't exist."

Jack strode back to the groundsman's shed and through the door. It remained closed. "Blasted door." He tried again. This time it flew open and he grinned when the boys stopped speaking to stare at it.

Kobe elbowed Xavier, grinning. "Told you it didn't mean he doesn't exist." Kobe started forward. "Come on." He left his school backpack by the door, Xavier doing the same.

Jack stepped to the side, watching as they made their way to the area behind the wardrobe, squeezing between it and the wall, both using their phones to light the way. He walked through the wardrobe, smiling as Xavier shifted from one foot to the other.

Kobe propped the cricket bat against the wall, in the corner. "We wanted to thank you." He slowly turned around, a wry smile appearing. "It feels odd not being able to see you."

Xavier placed the ball next to the bat. "Kobe said you used to play. Sometimes. Back when you were alive." He shrugged. "I don't know if you liked the game, but if you didn't, you can always ask the next person you help to get rid of them for you." He shrugged again. "Or they can use the bat to protect themselves."

Jack chuckled, wishing he could talk to them. "Thanks. They'll remind me of other times." His smile faded. Of the times before everything had fallen apart.

"I thought you might like a souvenir to remember us by," Kobe said. "Since the cops took the bat we left here."

"They've also kept quiet about what happened," Xavier said.

Kobe nodded. "Yeah. The principal said it was to protect our privacy since we're not adults. Neither of us believes that. Probably to stop rumours about the school. Some parents wouldn't want their kids here if they knew what had happened."

"Not that we're complaining," Xavier said. "We don't need people asking us to tell them everything about that night. We got enough of that from the cops."

"We were stuck answering questions for hours," Kobe said.

"Felt like we were the criminals," Xavier muttered.

Kobe grinned fleetingly. "It wasn't that bad. And we got out of a week of school. Although everyone fussing over us was annoying."

"Speak for yourself. My mum has been making my favourite meals all week," Xavier said.

"It's good to see you're both okay." Jack tried to push aside his anger at not being able to ask any of the questions he had. Why hadn't they been at school for a week? Had either of them been hurt?

"How about your mum not letting you go anywhere until yesterday when she dropped us at the footy game and my mum picked us up straight after?" Kobe asked.

"That part wasn't good, but I'm sure they'll ease off after a bit." Xavier grinned. "And we did meet those two girls."

"What girls?" Jack couldn't prevent himself from asking.

Kobe returned Xavier's grin before glancing around the area. "I took your advice, Jack. We're meeting up with them again next weekend. They're interested in some of the same things we like. Including cricket."

"That's good." Jack was glad life was going back to normal for them and they were moving past what had happened.

"They don't go to this school," Xavier said. "So we'll only get to see them on weekends."

Kobe nodded. "Yeah, we're not allowed to go

anywhere during the week and only supervised outings on the weekend."

"And school holidays," Xavier added.

"We've made plans to see them during the school holidays," Kobe said

"We were surprised we weren't permanently grounded," Xavier said. "Although I could have done without needing to go to a shrink every Wednesday afternoon."

"It's not that bad." Kobe shrugged. "We both have nightmares, but at least that means we survived."

"The nightmares aren't that bad," Xavier muttered.

When Kobe gave his friend a look, Jack chuckled. He was with Kobe on that matter. Xavier was bothered by them more than he was letting on.

"They aren't that bad," Xavier protested.

"Its okay, Xave. The nightmares are normal."

Jack's smile faded. He had his own nightmares to deal with. Ones he wouldn't wish on anyone even though sometimes it would have been nice to be able to share the burden of them with another.

"Yeah well, I hate them." Xavier looked towards the gap between the wardrobe and the wall. "We should probably go. Before classes start." He took a step backwards. "Thanks, Jack. Thanks for keeping us alive."

"I'm glad you lived." Jack watched Xavier slip past the wardrobe, turning his gaze to Kobe, who remained in the space behind the wardrobe. He wished he could ask him what he wanted. "Blasted bird."

Kobe stared straight ahead for a moment. "Thank you, Jack." He paused a moment. "You are better than Alvin. I hope you manage to atone for your sins and move on to wherever you're meant to go." He paused once again. "We wouldn't have made it through the night without you."

Jack watched Kobe leave, remaining behind the wardrobe as he listened to the retreating footsteps and the closing door. "I'm glad I could help." He wished he could have said the words to Kobe and Xavier. But he couldn't. It was back to days of being answered only by silence. Waiting until it was time to help the next student. For once that thought didn't bring with it annoyance and frustration. Or a touch of anger.

There'd be another one needing his help and so far he was doing okay. For such a major screw up he was actually managing to help. Was the angel as astonished as he was? Now that was something it wouldn't surprise him to learn was true. His gaze was drawn to the picture of Rose. His smile faded. The lives he'd saved couldn't make up for the ones he'd taken. Nothing could.

Free Ebook

Subscribe to Avril's newsletter and receive a free ebook. This ebook is exclusive to those on her mailing list. To find out more about this offer visit: www.avrilsabine.com/free-ebook

*

We value your privacy and will not sell, rent, exchange or loan your email address to third parties. Your information is confidential and you are under no obligation to remain on the mailing list and can unsubscribe at any time.

Acknowledgements

As always, all my thanks to my usual crew. Your help means a great deal and I appreciate all the work you do. For both the major and minor jobs. :)

To The Reader

If you enjoyed this book, why not consider leaving a review to help other readers discover it too? Reader engagement is one of the few ways that lets an author know readers want more books in a particular series or genre. So leave a review and tell friends, not only about this book but also about other ones you've enjoyed, so you can continue to enjoy books by your favourite authors for years to come.

Dreams are meant to be lived,

Avril.

About The Author

Avril is an Australian author who lives with her family on acreage in South East Queensland. She writes mostly young adult and children's speculative fiction, but has been known to dabble in other genres. You can find more information about her at www.avrilsabine.com where you can also subscribe to her newsletter to be kept informed about new releases, current projects, blog posts and exclusive news.

Titles By Avril Sabine

Stories about strong characters and characters who discover their strengths.

SERIES

Assassins Of The Dead- Young Adult Fantasy/ Paranormal

Book 1: Dark Blade

Book 2: Dragon Touched

Book 3: Society Against Vampires

Book 4: King's Request

Dragon Blood- Young Adult Urban Fantasy (with elements of romance)

(5 book series)

Book 1: Pliethin

Book 2: Wyvern

Book 3: Surety

Book 4: Knight

Book 5: Mage

Dragon Mage- Young Adult Urban Fantasy (with elements of romance)

(Series two of Dragon Blood series)

Book 1: Promise

Dragon Blood Chronicles- Young Adult Urban Fantasy (with elements of romance)

(Companion stand alone series to Dragon Blood)

Book 1: Oath

Book 2: Betrayed

Guardians Of The Round Table- Young Adult Fantasy LitRPG

(Co-written with Storm and Rhys Petersen)

Book 1: Dexterity Fail

Book 2: Goblin Boots

Book 3: Singed Feathers

Book 4: Frog Mage

Book 5: Crystal Mine

Book 6: Cursed Harp

Rosie's Rangers- Young Adult Western Steampunk

(6 book series)

Book 1: Justice

Book 2: Vengeance

Book 3: Treachery

Book 4: Accused

Book 5: Wanted

Book 6: Corruption

Mark Of Kings- Children's Fantasy

(Upper middle grade/preteen)

(4 book series)

Book 1: The Arena

Book 2: The Island

Book 3: The Assassin

Book 4: The King

STAND ALONE SERIES

Demon Hunters- Young Adult Urban Fantasy/ Horror (with elements of romance)

Book 1: Blood Sacrifice

Book 2: Retribution

Book 3: Tainted

Book 4: Premonition

Book 5: Cursed

Book 6: Feud

Book 7: Extrication

Plea Of The Damned- Young Adult Urban Fantasy/Paranormal

(6 book series)

Book 1: Forgive Me Lucy

Book 2: Forgive Me Aiden

Book 3: Forgive Me Jena

Book 4: Forgive Me Kobe

Book 5: Forgive Me Marti

Book 6: Forgive Me Dawson

Realms Of The Fae- Young Adult Urban Fantasy (with elements of romance)

The Sword (short story in Like A Girl Anthology)

Heart Of Stone

Book 1: A Debt Owed

Book 2: Marked By The Hunt

Book 3: The Magic Collector

Book 4: An Unexpected Betrayal

Book 5: Imprisoned By Iron

Fairytales Retold (Short Stories)

Snow-White And Rose-Red

The Twelve Brothers

The Light Princess

Beauty And The Beast

Sleeping Beauty

Aschenputtel

The Golden Bird

The Frog Prince

The Death Of Koshchei The Deathless

Myths And Legends Retold (Short Stories)

Ion, Son Of Apollo

Sir Gawain And The Maid With The Narrow Sleeves

Princess Ilse, The Giant's Daughter

YOUNG ADULT NOVELS

Young Adult Fantasy (with elements of romance)

Elf Sight

Earth Bound

Young Adult Urban Fantasy

Stone Warrior (with elements of romance)

The Jungle Inside

Young Adult Contemporary (with elements of romance)

Through Your Eyes

The Ugly Stepsister

Perfect Little Princess

Young Adult Contemporary/Paranormal

Whispers In The Dark (with elements of romance and same sex relationships)

Over Too Soon (with elements of romance)

Young Adult Sci-Fi

Experiment X-One-Six (Urban Sci-Fi/Superheroes)

An Endless Dawn (Post Apocalyptic Sci-Fi)

CHILDREN'S BOOKS

Dragon Lord (Preteen/early teens) (Fantasy)

The Irish Wizard (Upper middle grade) (Urban Fantasy)

SHORT STORIES

Urban Fantasy

Eternally Late

Dealings With Joe

Glimpses (short story in That Moment When Anthology)

Contemporary

The Brat Next Door

Fantasy LitRPG

(Set in the same world as Guardians Of The Round Table Series)

Tales Of Inadon 1: The Disc (Co-written with Storm and Rhys Petersen) (short story in Game On! Anthology)

Post Apocalyptic Sci-Fi

Compulsive Directive

NONFICTION

A Year Of Weekly Writing Exercises (Creative Writing)

Cooking For Families With Allergies (Cooking) (Co-written with Storm Petersen)

Tell Me A Story, Grandma (Memoir)

For the most up to date details on available titles visit:

www.avrilsabine.com/books/bibliography

Plea Of The Damned Series

To learn more about this series visit:

www.avrilsabine.com/series/potd

BOOKS AVAILABLE IN THE PLEA OF THE DAMNED SERIES:

Book 1: Forgive Me Lucy

Book 2: Forgive Me Aiden

Book 3: Forgive Me Jena

Book 4: Forgive Me Kobe

Book 5: Forgive Me Marti

Book 6: Forgive Me Dawson

Disclaimer

This is a work of fiction. Names, characters, businesses, places, events and incidents are either the products of the author's imagination or used in a fictitious manner. Any resemblance to actual persons, living or dead, or actual events is purely coincidental. The opinions expressed or beliefs held are those of the characters and should not be assumed to be the opinions or beliefs of the author.

www.ingramcontent.com/pod-product-compliance
Lightning Source LLC
Chambersburg PA
CBHW030834200726
48285CB00007B/2433